The critics cheer Elizabeth Crane's

When the Messenger Is Hot

"The women in Elizabeth Crane's stories are basket cases. . . . They are also smarter than they think they are, and funny. *When the Messenger Is Hot*, Crane's first collection, is mostly terrific. She writes wonderful, breathless run-ons, and when her characters tell their own stories, they speak in breakneck monologues. . . . Crane has a distinctive and eccentric voice that is consistent and riveting from the first story to the last, and *When the Messenger Is Hot* expresses a remarkably strong and coherent artistic vision."
— Jennifer Reese, *New York Times Book Review*

"Elizabeth Crane is a melancholy, hilarious writer whose first book has thoroughly ruffled the publishing world. . . . Crane is decidedly singular. . . . This is hardly chick lit: In fact, it's revolutionary fiction, both stylistically and thematically. . . . Taken as a whole, *When the Messenger Is Hot* is a kind of *Tibetan Book of the Alive*, a guide to those of us who have to stick around."
— Emily Gordon, *Newsday*

"Anyone who's read *Self-Help*, Lorrie Moore's debut collection, or *The Girls' Guide to Hunting and Fishing* by Melissa Bank will find something similar here: a cynical-but-poetic, laugh-out-loud sense of humor."
— Juliet Waters, *Montreal Mirror*

"This isn't just chick lit. . . . Crane's writing is vaguely reminiscent of Nick Hornby. Her stories are a little sad, but funny mostly, and real. . . . It's fascinating, that Crane could know so much about *you*. But she just does."
— Katie Millbauer, *Seattle Weekly*

"*When the Messenger Is Hot* avoids the trap of melancholy cuteness by sidestepping the conventions of the form. Instead of the usual third-person narrative overstuffed with meticulously collected images like a neurotic hobbyist's scrapbook, Crane offers up first-person tales that are fast-paced and conversational and rambling and frank. . . . A Crane protagonist is tough and opinionated but impulsive and self-destructive. She's vulnerable but honest, expressing her fear of appearing flawed even as she recognizes this is yet another flaw. She's on the brink of an epiphany, but she's too sharp to embrace her metamorphosis without ripping it to shreds first. . . . Crane has her finger on something here, an absurd human psyche that feeds on the words of girlfriends and therapists and friends in recovery, where self-esteem and bath salts are treated with equal solemnity. . . . As absurd or unhinged as Crane's characters' choices may be, we are not only coaxed into understanding why these characters make the choices they make; we agree with their choices, and we support them, in spite of ourselves. Instead of anticipating their demise with detachment, then, we're drawn into caring about these flawed women, even though we run a clear risk of getting hurt or being disappointed in the process — which is exactly the kind of courage that Crane's characters strive for, and the kind of courage she reflects in creating such a boldly original collection."
— Heather Havrilesky, *Washington Post Book World*

"Marvelously keyed-up and jittery narratives. . . . Crane's breathless stories hit the brain with more voltage than a double espresso." — *Booklist*

"Hilariously off-kilter. . . . In a day and age when drug companies advertise a pill for every pain, there's something utterly refreshing about the way Crane's narrators bareback their way through life's rough spots, pharmaceutical free, refusing easy closure. . . . In the hilarious title piece, Crane dramatizes the exhausting mental gymnastics a woman goes through by simply thinking about going on a date."
— John Freeman, *San Francisco Chronicle*

"*When the Messenger Is Hot* is so delightful. The women in Crane's stories may be a little off-kilter (what with their rehab and their hopeless love affairs), but they're clever, original, and kind of silly about it all. Never self-indulgent or whiny. (Imagine!)" — DailyCandy.com

"Crane's voice is sharp and smart and wholly sympathetic. . . . There's an energy and immediacy to these stories that make them feel as if they could have been delivered in one beautiful, raw rant over a bottle of wine."
— Karen Valby, *Entertainment Weekly*

"I've often wondered where exactly I could find the 'fringes of society.' Then I read these stories. . . . The voice is so damn clever it made me think the fringe might not be such a bad place to visit." — Lori Yacovone, *Jane*

"Though Crane's stories deal with serious issues — love, dishonesty, betrayal, grief, drinking, sadness — her tone displays polish, humor, and a delectable lightness. . . . This is the perfect Valentine's day bonbon for people whose romantic histories can most charitably be described as checkered." — Deirdre Donahue, *USA Today*

"The clever, caustic Elizabeth Crane is simply too good to pass unmentioned. . . . So strong and charming is Crane's voice, so mordant and goofy and unique is her sensibility." — Darcy Cosper, *Bookforum*

"The women in Elizabeth Crane's stories never shut up. Ever. At least not to you. To friends and lovers and parents the voice is probably less garrulous, less confiding, less honest in assessing life's absurdities. But you, the reader, are the confessor. You will hear it all: the bad boyfriends, the job difficulties, the terrifying crises of identity, the heart-wrenching loss of parents, and, of course, more bad boyfriends. . . . What's most remarkable about Crane's wry, deliberately absurd tales is their overwhelming current of sorrow. Crane may hit the funny bone more often than not, but she's secretly taking dead aim at the heart." — Connie Ogle, *Miami Herald*

"The stories in this collection are strangely moving evocations of how it's possible to be both smart and dumb, wise and clueless, lost and found." — Sara Nelson, *Glamour*

"The world Elizabeth Crane presents is a planet tilted slightly, jauntily on its axis. . . . *When the Messenger Is Hot* sets out a unique, intriguing, and often hilarious vision. Crane's heroines have been around the block a few times but still have tread on their tires and an off-key song in their hearts. The world they're given to navigate is unpredictable, the fates capricious, the winds tricky, and yet they press forward, holding on to their hats. I haven't seen women quite like them anywhere else."
— Carol Anshaw, *Chicago Tribune*

"The messenger may be hot, but Elizabeth Crane is hotter. . . . Sharp, distinctive, and wickedly funny, *When the Messenger Is Hot* is a terrific debut collection. . . . The stories are edgy without that "look-I'm-being-edgy" self-awareness; they are touching without cloying sentimentality. . . . Crane dredges up almost every clichéd character trait from the chick-lit genre and skewers it to the wall."   — Rebecca Swain Vadnie, *Orlando Sentinel*

"*When the Messenger Is Hot* is a fireball of the imagination, a whopper of a debut, a quiet stunner. At first, Crane lulls readers with sentences that never end, with thoughts that twist and turn into unexpected corners, and it seems as if you are sitting in a Starbucks on a city corner (usually Chicago but not always) listening in on someone's private thoughts. Then the turns become more surreal and before you know it you are laughing until you cry or crying until you laugh — it's hard to say which."
— Mindi Dickstein, *St. Petersburg Times*

When the Messenger Is Hot

Stories

Elizabeth Crane

BACK BAY BOOKS
Little, Brown and Company
BOSTON   NEW YORK   LONDON

Originally published in hardcover by Little, Brown
and Company, January 2003
First Back Bay paperback edition, January 2004

The characters and events in this book are fictitious.
Any similarity to real persons, living or dead,
is coincidental and not intended by the author.

Grateful acknowledgment is made to the following publications
in which some of these stories were first published:
"Christina," *Bridge Magazine;* "Return from the Depot!" *New York Stories;*
"The Archetype's Girlfriend," *Washington Square;* "The Daves,"
Book Magazine; "The Super Fantastic New Zealand Triangle,"
Sycamore Review; "Something Shiny," *Chicago Reader.*
Adam Langer's article "When the Writer Is Hot," which is
reprinted in the reading group guide at the back of this book,
first appeared in the *Chicago Tribune Magazine* on January 26, 2003.
Copyright © 2003 by the Chicago Tribune. Reprinted with permission.
Elizabeth Crane's essay "On the Subject of Influences Blatant, Less Blatant,
Random, or Otherwise," which is reprinted in the reading group guide
at the back of this book, first appeared at Powells.com.
Reprinted with permission.

Library of Congress Cataloging-in-Publication Data

Crane, Elizabeth.
   When the messenger is hot : stories / Elizabeth Crane. — 1st ed.
      p. cm.
   ISBN 0-316-09652-0 (hc) / 0-316-60846-7 (pb)
      1. United States — Social life and customs — 20th century — Fiction.
   2. Women — United States — Fiction.   I. Title.

PS3603.R38 W47 2002
813'.6 — dc21   2002024182

10   9   8   7   6   5   4   3   2

Book design by Robert G. Lowe

Q-FF

Printed in the United States of America

for Mom, in memory,
and for Dad,

with love

Contents

When
the Messenger
Is Hot

The Archetype's Girlfriend

SARAH OR ANYA OR MAX is five foot ten, five foot nine or five foot eight, but never shorter, and she's naturally thin. She's thirty or she's twenty, or she's almost forty and looks ten years younger even when she rolls out of bed in the morning. She's not a flawless beauty, but you think she is, and she has perfect skin and wears no makeup, or she won't leave the house without eyebrow pencil and blood-red lipstick, her trademark. Her hair is dark with short bangs, or it changes lengths and colors several times during the course of the year or three or nine months you're together, or it's long and thick and curly and when you tell her never to cut it, she goes into the bathroom with your clippers to cut it down to a quarter inch because she won't be told what to do by a man and when she's done you fuck each other hard on the bathroom floor. Her panties and bras match, or she doesn't wear a bra because her whatever-size breasts are perfectly proportioned and she hates the constriction of underwires. She shaves every bit of hair off her body, or she doesn't shave her armpits or her bikini line because it is a subversion of femininity to do so, and after your first month together, during which time you're decidedly uncertain about your own female body hair policy, you come to defend this point of view when it arises in conversation, without mentioning names. She wears a tiny four-hundred-dollar cashmere sweater she pilfered from a photo shoot with inside-out sweatpants and manages to make it look sexy, or she wears a striped sleeve for a hat that on anyone else you would be forced to call into question, or if she has any money she wears tight black pants with heels and a dry-cleaned white blouse with a pearl choker, and she has tattoos that only a few people will see, or a pierced clitoris, and if you ever tell her an outfit looks cute, she will change. You leave work to make love to her in the kitchen, or you skip work to drive to some motel and stop at a phone booth on the tollway instead because you can't make it that far, or you quit your bartending job entirely because it's interfering with your mutual need to have hourly sex, or you only make love a few times early on because she has issues, which you think you will cure her of by doing everything possible to please her, which you don't, and you go to therapy together a few times, where a pinched-looking woman tells you it's no one's fault, but you will still take it personally.

In high school she got effortless straight A's and constantly complained about the incompetence of the faculty, or she ditched to smoke pot in the park and talk about the books that ought to be on the required-reading list. When she was three her hippie parents finally got married, wearing flowers in their hair and matching embroidered dresses, or by the time she was eight she loathed her blue-collar parents for bringing children into a cesspool of wood paneling and avocado appliances, or she came from such old Upper East Side money that no one recalled where it came from and wouldn't speak of it even if they did because it was improper, and went to Brearley for twelve long years but hated it and her parents by the time she was fourteen, when she went from wearing Carter's to wearing no underpants at all underneath her school uniform. When her parents were married, they had sex loudly and all the time, and talked openly about it, or it never took place at all and was not discussed until the time of her first abortion in her sophomore year, at which time her father was heard to say to her mother, *Pay by cash*, and nothing more. When they were divorced her mother had a series of lovers, or she developed a fondness for prescription pills, or she remarried immediately, to a man who had no known record of employment or social security number, who touched Sarah or Anya or Max in an inappropriate sexual manner conveniently short of anything criminal. She had an affair with the newly graduated physics teacher in her junior year, or when she was a senior she fucked a sophomore in the boys' locker room, and she had no long-term friendships to speak of, or a best girlfriend she experimented with sexually and picked fights with after breaking their plans on a rare Saturday night when she didn't have a date.

She went to Harvard or Wesleyan or graduated early from Bennington, where she had a string of openly lesbian affairs but refused to define her sexuality as gay, straight, or bi, all of the above being limiting, or she broke up the marriage of her rhetoric professor and immediately thereafter left him for a mechanic she lived with for a year, who she subsequently left for a guy she bummed a cig off of at a poetry reading. She majored in comparative literature or Eastern philosophy and graduated with honors, or quit with one semester left to join the Israeli army.

She's been in graduate school for five years, waiting tables and working on her thesis on the deconstruction of aesthetic preconceptions in Dadaism, or she sells dresses made from tarot cards on the corner

6

of Houston and Lafayette, or she's a freelance stylist who prior to you dated mostly indie rock stars with a penchant for heroin, or she makes a fortune in advertising but complains bitterly about how she's sold out and should have stayed in art school, but can't break her addiction to Kate Spade bags and anything from Kiehl's. She's been engaged three times and still has all the rings, or she's been married in the eyes of god but doesn't feel the need to prove anything with meaningless papers or rings, and she has ended every relationship she's been in. She's had more than one abortion, which she'll mention but not discuss, or she refers to her *hospitalization* with little detail except to say it was *a mistake* and the reason she lost custody of her only daughter, and she's manic or depressive, but never both. She has stacks of identical black hardbound notebooks festooned with band stickers or cigarette burns, and she spends hours filling them with ideas or feelings or drawings, or poetry that on the rare occasion she decides to share, will go over your head or be worse than bad, but you won't say so, and you are probably so blindly in love that you won't realize it either way. She listens to Hole or Björk or Liz Phair, or she describes Liz Phair as *polite* and says that there aren't any female artists who haven't sold out, and listens to some kind of noise that she plays passionately for you and tries to explain in detail, and you will listen patiently to both the explanation and the alleged music as one or the other drives a power tool through your brain, and she will make love to you after this, but it might hurt. Or she has a subscription to the opera, which would cause you to want to die tragically before the tenor has a chance to, were it not for the fact that she invites you to masturbate her during some critical aria.

She drives a rusty pale blue Dodge Dart and knows how to adjust the timing, which gives you a hard-on just thinking about it, or she drives a brand-new BMW and makes excuses about it, or her license has been suspended for a year because of three speeding tickets but she's still driving around anyway. At dinner she eats meat and always orders an appetizer and dessert, or she's been a vegetarian since she was seventeen because the sacrifice of animals is inhumane, but she wears a curly lamb coat because it's vintage and chain-smokes Marlboros. Her stuff is in storage because she was traveling in Turkey for six months, or if she has an apartment, you can't see the floor through the clothes, or there are books piled up everywhere, and it smells like cigarettes and patchouli and dog. There's a beaded curtain somewhere and lots of religious candles, or unstretched mostly black paintings on the walls and an Indian-cotton bedspread thumbtacked over the window, and it's a one-bedroom she shares with a guy she used to have sex with, or it's an all-white loft the size of a football field with nothing in it but a bed and track lighting and dozens of mammoth paintings given to her by artist friends, some of which are hung but most of which are leaned up against the wall like records, one in front of another, and when you become absorbed in one of the numerous portraits of her, she says, *I don't really like that,* in such a way that actually makes your heart hurt for the ex-lover who painted it. She moves in with you at the end of your second date and makes you think it was your idea.

You meet when she slam-dances into you at the Mudd Club, or at a gas station where she's shoving and cursing at a guy twice her size who kicked his pit bull she's locked inside her Jeep, or when you go to pick up dog food at the groomer's, where she's got a squirrelly Pomeranian on a steel table, a pair of shears in one hand, a comb in the other, and a cigarette dangling from her lips. You talk all night and discover that you share favorite obscure authors, or that she has a passion for monster trucks or wild game, which causes you to propose immediately with absolute naive sincerity and her to cavalierly toss her head back in laughter because you do not yet know that she has been proposed to countless times in a similar manner, and you make love from 8 A.M. until noon in ways you never imagined possible, or you dry hump with all your clothes on and ejaculate prematurely for which you are sensitively forgiven, or forgiven with a Mona Lisa look on her face that you choose to interpret as sensitive, but might not be.

You love her because she can talk about cars or dogs or wild game or politics, about which she has a point of view that you may or may not agree with, and because she never asks what you're feeling, for which she is exalted until you realize that this is because she isn't about to tell you either. You love her bras in your bathroom and her cigarette butts in your beer cans, or her pearls and tap pants on your kitchen floor. You love that her dog has gone to obedience school and she loves your unsuppressed instinct to heel when she's actually giving commands to the dog. You love when she uses your razor or drinks Jack Daniel's from the bottle, or watching her masturbate, which she does frequently. You love the way she laughs from deep in her throat, or watching her pull her split ends apart, or that she throws a softball overhand. You love her because she will agree to a drive across country with a moment's notice, or she will invite a girlfriend to join you in fulfilling your ultimate fantasy of a three-way, which you will chicken out on, or she'll try mushrooms with you on a camping trip. You adore her because everything that's attractive about her seems accidental, when in fact there is always some presence of calculation, or at least an awareness that a centimeter of her pale belly is visible between her ribbed turtleneck and her Levi's, or that you've been watching her masturbate since the beginning.

What she does that drives you mad is she calls her mother daily and tells her everything, everything, or she hasn't spoken to either of her parents in years, but refuses to mitigate this choice by seeking help, or perhaps talking to you, or she changes the code on her voice mail so that you can't access it, and seems to be checking it more often, or when you start hearing "you've got mail" more times a day than the total number of friends you have combined even though she previously decried the insidiousness of the Internet, and casually defends herself by saying she's catching up with an old friend, which will cause you to spend many hours illuminated only by the light of your laptop trying to no avail to crack her voice-mail code, her e-mail code, her bank code, any kind of code that will provide you with some glint of information about the woman you have been living with who you fantasize is an international spy because the only other explanation is that the only woman you will ever love, the woman to whom all future women will be compared (unfavorably), is obviously a stranger. You stop short of stalking, because you're slightly more stable than that and because she lives in your house, but she will have a full-on mental breakdown if you try to define your relationship, or if you take thirty minutes instead of ten to bring back a pack of Camels, which is around the time when you notice that she starts to notice the bartender at P & G, or after an argument she spends a night at her girlfriend's when you know she doesn't have even one, and afterward unashamedly admits to sleeping with someone else but says it didn't mean anything, or that it did, and she's leaving you. She breaks up with you because she's in love with the lead singer of a band you've never heard of and she hopes you'll try to understand because she's never felt this way about anyone before and you've been really important to her but she won't say how or why and you suddenly and tragically realize this is the most heartfelt expression of feelings she's ever offered you, or because the way your towel on the bed day after day is causing her to slowly lose her mind, or for no reason at all, but she is always the one who decides. You don't date at all for an entire year after your breakup, or you have a series of short-term relationships with nice girls you just aren't in love with, or you move in with a sous chef you really do care about but don't go to any great lengths to hide the one blurry photo of your happy minute with Sarah or Anya or Max, and almost break up with Jenny or Katie or Sue over the detritus you refuse to discard even after the ultimatum. Your chance at redemption occurs three or five or ten years later when you and Jenny or Katie or Sue run into Sarah or Anya or Max at the P & G, where you haven't been since before she broke up with you, and she's still gorgeous but looks really tired flirting with the new bartender, or when you run into her just after your play got nominated for an Obie and she tells you she's almost finished with her thesis, or she just filed for bankruptcy after no one bought her fall line of sleeve hats, but the deliverance fails because in spite of knowing better you can't help thinking of Sarah or Anya or Max when Jenny or Katie or Sue turns up a Hootie or Basia or Jewel song on the car radio, or because you're just a decent enough guy not to fully enjoy someone else's pathetic life, even if it is the girlfriend who ruined yours.

Something Shiny

SO GET THIS: they're going to make a movie of my life.

I could kind of care less about the movie, but I figure this is probably my only chance to win an Oscar, which I've dreamed about since I was in seventh grade. Really, I just want to wear the jewels and maybe a simple tiara and have the chance to say, *It's Prada.* Actually, it would be fine just to be nominated, even if I was in one of those categories that doesn't get televised that they show all at once in a quick montage in the kind of slow two hours in the middle of the show. I don't really have any desire to be famous. I'd just like to have something shiny with my name on it to leave behind. Anyway, I hadn't ever given a lot of thought to exactly how to do that, not being an actress or a director or anything related to that at all, but then all these crappy things happened and I wrote a book about it (a *memoir* they call it, even though I'm in my thirties and it seems a bit premature in spite of the events) and made sure to work it out in the fine print that I'd be able to write the screenplay as well. I realize it's a long shot.

So yesterday I get this message on my machine saying, *Hi, this is Apple Fowler and you may have already heard I'm going to be playing the part of Wendy in the film version of* No But Wait, It Gets Worse . . . , *and I was hoping I could talk to you about it* . . . and so on. Very bizarre to hear someone refer to you as a "part," like you're either fictional, or not whole. To be honest, Apple Fowler is a good enough actress, but she's kind of young to be playing me even where the book starts. I guess I shouldn't be surprised. Anyway, I call her back, and she's really nice, much nicer than you'd expect a movie star to be, and asks if she can come over for coffee. So we make plans and she comes over and asks me a lot of questions and looks around my apartment like it's this curiosity, like it's somehow different from any other average person's apartment, which I suppose maybe she hasn't had access to as the child of a famous director. It seems like she's never seen a houseplant or a refrigerator magnet or, um, a dog. Still, she's easy to talk to and seems genuinely interested in getting to know me and says that she loved the book and can't even begin to imagine how I made it through everything, and I'm sure she can't, given that she seems a little weirded out by my average-person's apartment, which isn't on the long list of things I personally consider myself to have made it through. Anyway, she eventually asks if she can stay for a week or so, to really *become* the character, and she offers to pay me rent, which isn't an issue since my book's been on the bestseller list for eight weeks, and I've got plenty of room, plus, I mean, who wouldn't want to be friends with Apple Fowler? Maybe she knows George Clooney's e-mail address. I agree with the condition that the bathroom is mine first and the phone is off-limits, which isn't a problem for her since she's got a cell phone, and also because she says she really wants to *experience* my life and intends to use the phone for emergencies only. She says she'll be as quiet as a mouse.

Which she is, and she sticks by her thing not to even use her own phone, but right away I realize that it's not an awful lot of fun being watched, which I suppose is what the readers are doing in a certain way, except they're not in my house. The first day or two she just takes a lot of notes. It's immediately bizarre to me to see someone writing something down when

I'm in the middle of doing something absolutely mundane, something that as a writer I hadn't previously considered was worth writing down, like hand-washing a sweater, which of course is not something Apple has ever witnessed, which perhaps would seem even more unusual to a nonchore-oriented person when followed by using a tweezer to pry out the sink stopper, which broke ages ago, one of those numerous daily adjustments I stopped thinking about as anything that even needs a repair, like the way I play my answering machine messages back on my stereo because the machine records messages but won't play them back, or the way I serve Leo (my pug) his Alpo out of my Chrysler Building mug on the sofa every night because he won't eat until I'm eating, and he won't even eat on the floor by the table because it's too far from me, which I personally think is really considerate on his part, and therefore I do not mind fixing him his dinner in my Chrysler Building mug seeing as how he's so obviously trying to keep me company, all of which Apple scribbles down as somehow being crucial and noteworthy character traits.

After the watching and the note-taking, she starts trying to imitate me — my gestures, facial expressions, my voice. I think she's sort of got it, but what do I know? It's not like I ever studied myself. But you think you know how you seem to people, and you really don't. I think of myself as unremarkable in a lot of ways; I don't have a New York accent, and I don't think I have any overly weird habits like not letting my food touch on the plate or being especially neat or sloppy, although I am sometimes afflicted by a tiny bit of obsessive-compulsive disorder when it comes to locking my door; I usually have to unlock it and lock it again to make sure it's locked, and I tend to check it a bunch of times before I go to bed, too, which obsession has not gone past Apple, but so anyway she manages to find interest in the way I shuffle my slippered feet and in my fairly rigid schedule of having frozen donut holes and 1 percent milk in bed when *Seinfeld* comes on at 7:30 (Leo joins at the foot of the bed with a Milk-Bone), which I notice because she shuffles her slippered feet over to my bed with her own donut holes and milk (and Milk-Bone) before I have a chance to get there first. I do end up letting her chip in when she asks to use my shampoo and conditioner and pretty much all of my products. It may be equally as fascinating to me that she thinks using my shampoo has some relevance to the Wendy experience as it probably is to her that I use generic shampoo. Anyway, she goes as far as getting her hair cut like mine (by my haircutter) even though her hair is poker straight and mine takes forty-five minutes to blow out and still needs to be slept on for a night if I don't want to look like an extra on *Dynasty*. She wants to know where I got my purple camouflage pants and all my little beaded cardigans (which I'm sort of known for) and has never heard of eBay, so I sit her down at the computer and take some bit of time to explain to her how the Internet works, and when we finally get into eBay, although she's completely willing to out-and/or overbid for any item by a ridiculous amount, she doesn't want to wait for the auctions to end, so we venture out to get her some sweaters, which I wouldn't have minded so much if she weren't a size two. Those cardigans tend to be on the small side (I don't know if women were smaller in the fifties or what), and she ends up with a spectacular midnight blue one I could never have gotten one arm into, but I try to keep my resentment to myself; she was just born that way.

Naturally, I don't ever drive around New York City, but Apple has a car and knows from the book that I lived in L.A. for a while (after a fight with my then-boyfriend I got on a plane in an alcoholic black-out, and even though I sobered up about a week later I wasn't in any big rush to get back to New York) and that driving was this huge deal (and I'm not even go-ing to discuss the whole matter of buying a used car in L.A., which is a trauma I just don't have the time to get into), suddenly having to drive everywhere, driv-ing a mile even just to get milk (and then it's some gi-ant Ralph's where the milk is of course in the back and you have to walk three city blocks through the store to get it so that the total milk-errand time is never less than forty-five minutes), but also having to drive 37.4 miles to and from work every day, not to mention the many thousands of dollars spent on auto repair totaling more than the actual cost of my car. I lived in L.A. for four years and never got comfortable driving. And so Apple asks me to take her for a ride in her Expedition, which to me is the equivalent of driving the Broadway bus, and we go on a short, rectangular route (all right turns) up Riverside Drive to 107th Street, back down West End Avenue, and home, which is going to have to be enough for her to observe my driving weirdnesses, which apparently it is, because she finds it noteworthy that I keep both hands on the wheel at all times (at "ten and two," isn't that the law?) and can only change radio stations at a red light and cannot do anything like change a tape or drink something (*Even with a cup holder and a straw?* she asks) and of course would never even consider trying to use a cell phone. She also makes note of my Tourette's-like swearing at any car that comes within three feet of the perimeter of our car, which is of course pretty much constantly, and I tell her that that trait was genetically passed on to me by my mother, who makes creative use of the word *cock* in any number of unpleasant driving scenarios. Apple then makes the same loop and has to correct herself a few times when she's inclined to zap a Ricky Martin song while in motion, but quickly gets the cursing down and by the time we get back has also incorporated other small gestures, like the way I shake my watch down toward my wrist when it gets too tight and the way I wear my sunglasses on top of my head to keep the hair out of my face but then squint the whole time, and I begin to feel a little uncomfortable, wishing I were some perfectly generic, gestureless individual.

Which is apparently not true according to my friend Sue, who calls later that day when I'm out picking up a quart of milk and is still on the phone with Apple when I walk in. Apple looks a little guilty and apologizes to me for picking up the phone by *force of habit* and tells Sue to hold on and passes the phone to me, but when I say hello, she says, *I think we have a bad connection. I have to go anyway, I'll call you tomorrow*, even though I can hear her perfectly fine. Apple seems pleased with how easily she was able to convince Sue that she was me, but I've been mistaken for other people on the phone plenty of times and I try not to make too much of it this time.

Day three she asks me a lot of questions about when it was that I started drinking and why, since the book starts right after I got out of rehab, and some of this is covered in the book, but when I started drinking, it was just this complete sense of rightness with the world. Maybe some people feel that way naturally, maybe some other people talk with Jesus, I don't know. How I've stayed sober is as much a mystery to me as to anyone. I had just celebrated ninety days of sobriety when my boyfriend broke up with me and at that point I still wanted to drink pretty much every day. But I had already enrolled in grad school for a doctorate in philosophy (also in a blackout, although it turned out to be a better idea than most of the ones I came up with while unconscious), which, although a debatable program, given future job prospects, gave me something more constructive to do than sit around and contemplate the leak in my ceiling. (Which, trust me, is not a metaphor, neither the leak nor its subsequent contemplation.) I didn't have a job at the time, and the thought of getting one was kind of horrifying. Apple asks a lot of questions I'm not sure I really have answers for. It's not as though I'm some Olympic triumph-over-tragedy story with violin music playing in the background as I discuss the nature of my faith in god and explain that I believe that there was some mystical reason I survived being hit by a car going forty-five miles an hour on Wilshire Boulevard (I was *walking;* I was in a very bad drunk-walking accident and I'm sure I crossed against the light, not to mention that there aren't even a lot of sober pedestrians in L.A., and I'm sure the driver who hit me was not at fault in any way) without anything more than a scraped knee, this after landing in front of a Starbucks that was a good half block from the site of impact. It wasn't until after I ordered a double espresso that I happened to notice the totaled Lexus still in the middle of the street; some people in the Starbucks were asking me if I was okay, which I thought was odd since there was a totaled Lexus in the street that might have someone dead in it (it didn't; the driver had only minor injuries) and they told me that the totaled Lexus had just hit me, to which I think I said something like, *Really,* because of course I had no memory of anything before the double espresso. Anyway, the point is that while it was undoubtedly the first time I noticed that fairly bad things happened when I drank, I didn't quit drinking because I suddenly thought I was called to go on some drunk-walking lecture circuit, or because some clouds parted and Hello Kitty told me to carry a message of love and tolerance and rebirth, or because some other upper-level spiritual message came to me which I can't really even make up an imaginary example of, that's how ridiculous I think that is. I'm pretty much of the I Have No Fucking Idea school of why the hell this has all gone down. Whether god hates me or loves me or is involved in other things entirely, I have no idea. I've run into more than a few people on the book tour who've had experiences similar to or worse than mine who tell me the particular ways they've stayed sober, which usually involve a very particular god idea I either can't comprehend or don't want to comprehend, like god speaking to them through their dog or whatever (although I have a close personal relationship with Leo, I am 100 percent certain that he is just a dog and not a deity of any kind), and I always nod politely, but the truth is I'm looking into their black eyes and thinking nobody's home. I'm sure that a lot of people just get to a point where they realize they don't have answers for certain things and so they just tell themselves these little lies so that they can make sense of some senseless things, whereas personally I'm not so inclined to be 100 percent certain that there's even a sun in the sky (which is not unrelated to the whole philosophy-study thing), but what I do know is I wasn't built with that switch, otherwise I might have skipped the booze. There's not a second of my day that goes by that I can avoid the awareness that I'm different, and the best I can do now is try to blend in and hope no one notices.

Anyway so Apple asks a few questions about my love life and looks like she's about to cry when I tell her I felt at my absolute loneliest when I was in love the one time (not the same prerehab ex; in hindsight I don't know how to describe that other than as a hostage situation), and I guess I don't do a very good job of explaining, since she does seem to understand that we were right for each other but not the part about why I broke it off. Maybe I'm not so sure myself. I know I lose Apple somewhere in the middle of this story, but anyway, she listens to all this and looks at me empathetically but in that way that you know she has no resources to draw upon for this "part," and look, I don't wish these resources on anyone.

She practically begs to come along to my regular A.A. meeting, which I explain is not open to nonalcoholics, and I try to emphasize the word *anonymous* in some way that will make her grasp its meaning. I give her a schedule of some meetings that are also open to nonalcoholics. But she shows up at my meeting a few minutes after it starts and raises her hand and says, *Hi, I'm Wendy and I'm an alcoholic,* and proceeds to share about how much gratitude she has for her sobriety and how her life is very small (oh really?) and that in spite of the difficulties that *most of you* know about, the promises of A.A. have really come true for her and that she has found an inner peace, and for the first time feels fully present in her life one day at a time. Like I'd ever say anything so cheesy. And then, as if it isn't enough that she's stolen my name and my difficulties, some of my friends go up to her after the meeting and tell her how great she looks, that she seems really well rested and more open or something, and they ask her to go to coffee at Utopia as though she's me, as though I weren't actually there in plain sight, as though someone who weighs easily forty pounds less than I do and who has an obvious nose job and a tattoo around her wrist and *is a movie star* is the same person they've known for nine years. I finally walk over to the group and I go, *Um, hello? Did we have a vote that it's okay to drop acid in Alcoholics Anonymous today? Because you seem not to be able to tell the difference between me and Apple Fowler* . . . And my friend Josh goes, *Did you hear something just now?* and my friend Sue goes, *Something kind of mumbly,* and my friend Missy goes, *A little bit like the grown-ups on Charlie Brown,* and Josh goes, *Wohwohwohwoh wooooh,* and everyone laughs like nothing unusual is going on. Then Sue looks right at me and puts on some lipstick as though she's confused me with a compact, and I rush to the ladies' room to see that I look the same as always but as I'm walking away I notice in the reflection that the shape of me matches the ancient wallpaper that's peeling off the walls, and so I move to a section of the wall that's painted that kind of icky pea green and I see that the shape of me is now pea green, and when a woman comes out of the stall I touch her arm and say to her, *Excuse me,* and I'm about to ask if I look all right to her but she sort of looks past me and brushes her arm like she has an itch and then walks away. My friends are already gone when I go back to the meeting room and I notice that I'd been standing in front of a shiny new filing cabinet when Sue was putting on her lipstick, but I still feel sure it wasn't the cabinet she was using as a mirror.

Of course, as I walk away I plan to tell Apple I know I said she could stay longer but I really need my privacy now and that she needs to leave, but when I get home her stuff is already gone, which is a great relief to me since I'm not very good at confronting people. There's a giant houseplant and a note that says, "Thanks so much for sharing yourself with me." I do freak out for about five minutes because Leo doesn't come running to the door to greet me, during which time I become certain Apple's taken him too, but I finally find him sleeping next to my bed. I have eight messages on my machine, which is highly unusual, and I take the tape out and play them back on the stereo and there are messages from Sue and Missy and Josh saying how happy they are to see me doing so well now and there are a few more from some other friends of mine who seem to think I've talked to them recently, which I haven't, and worst of all, messages from my sister and my ex, both saying how great it was to see me and how much lighter I seem (I think they mean this metaphorically) and my ex has that phone voice I haven't heard since a few months before we broke up, that sex voice. Leo refuses dinner on the sofa, and when he finally eats, it's not very much, and it's on the floor, like normal dogs, and he continues to act generally mopey for a while.

And then don't you know the next day in the supermarket I get to the checkout line and there's a picture of Apple holding hands with my ex-boyfriend under a headline reading, "Apple Fowler's New Mystery Man," and if that isn't bad enough, the checker thinks I'm a shelf of Wrigley's spearmint gum and I have to go home and order all my groceries all over again from the Internet, which is obviously, at this point, the least of my problems.

I continue to go to my A.A. meeting for a while, but people mistake me for a broken chair or an exhaust vent and every time I try to share, all they hear is a muffled noise and they just ask everyone else to speak a little louder. For a few months I try to phone my friends, but it's the same thing every time, *Hello, hello?* and they hang up. My e-mails all come back to me, although for some reason the landlord and the utilities still like my money and most Internet businesses seem to have no problem accepting my credit cards, which I guess isn't so surprising, and so I order everything that way.

It was sort of disorienting at first, to put it mildly, living this way. Leo finally came around after he realized Apple wasn't coming back, but I'd be lying if I said we were as close as we once were. I still go out to the park sometimes, or to the museums, since you can obviously get in free when you pass for a Picasso, but I was starting to feel like I was in a bad horror movie and I did think about messing with people's heads or robbing banks or something but it's not really in me and I never did get interested in taking advantage of my . . . well, I don't even know what I am now. I'm not invisible. I'm sort of just hidden. Like a chameleon, but without the taste for insects. So finally I just gave up hoping I'd be seen and decided to stay in most of the time. Which, to be honest, is not a dramatic change in lifestyle.

So Apple makes the movie and it gets rave reviews, movie of the year and all that, and she's on the cover of every magazine and gets nominated for best actress but I am of course overlooked for the screenwriting credit or any kind of credit; it seems all but forgotten that this movie is about a real person's life, but apparently Apple Fowler is better at being me than me because not only does she show up on the red carpet wearing a tiara and my Prada dress, she actually wins the Oscar, wins the Oscar for being me, and she bursts into tears and thanks her higher power and her agent and my sister and her *fiancé* my exboyfriend, who is naturally also weeping in the audience, and she's America's sweetheart and she's Apple Fowler again and there is something shiny with my name on it but there's still no me.

Privacy and Coffee

ONE DAY MY RICH FRIEND ANNA said, *Oh next time you come to New York we can go up to the solarium it's so beautiful and quiet and no one's ever there and you can write and have privacy and coffee.* Anna knew perfectly well how much New York caused me to go kind of mental (like being on an IV drip of crack cocaine), hence my having moved away, and Anna's a very thoughtful person, and so knowing this, when I did have to come, family obligations and all that, she was, I'm sure, just trying to make me as comfortable as possible under the circumstances. Got me milk and cookies and Raisin Bran and coffee and the right kind of cream and those Kleenex tissues with aloe, and a bigger TV. A few days into the visit

(picture one of those films where everything is accel-
erated and the person is seen only as a blur of light,
moving from place to place almost as though they're
on a track, with some weird implication that they
have no control over their course), Anna said again,
Let me show you the solarium, you'll love it, so I
grabbed my notebook and she brought me upstairs,
even though the elevator man said, *I see nothing,* in
some vaguely Eastern European accent, because theoretically you're only supposed to access the solarium
by going down to the lobby and back up an elevator
bank in the opposite section of the building, so as not
to disturb the Chihuahuas on the twentieth floor in
Anna's section, who, apparently, were in the middle of
being sued for barking inappropriately, and I guess
the idea was that we not bring any new lawsuits
against the dogs by causing them to bark when we
walked by their door to enter the stairwell to the roof.
Which they did, and which Chihuahua owner gave us
some particularly rude looks, as though we were the
ones doing the barking. Plus there was a sign with
bold red letters on the door, one of those official ones
carved into a big piece of wood paneling, that read DO
NOT OPEN DOOR ALARM WILL SOUND, which I didn't
even notice, and Anna seemed to know was a big fat
lie, because in fact no sound was heard except for the
fading cries of the Chihuahuas.

So we opened the door at the top of the stairs and

came out onto this indescribably huge terrace, which was about three times as big as my apartment back in Chicago, and I want to say that to me, as a New Yorker, my apartment in Chicago is pretty big. Obviously it's nothing like Anna's. Anna and I both have two bedrooms, but on Central Park West, you know, my two-bedroom could fit into her living room. Still, when I left New York, my studio apartment had no windows, literally. They weren't sealed or facing a brick wall: there were none. I guess the landlord figured what's the point, since they would have been facing a brick wall if there had been any, and why lie? In Chicago, I grow plants. I sit on the porch. There aren't so many people out on the street. There's less pressure. I'm not saying I go out a lot to verify that. It's just that when I lived in New York in the window-free apartment, I pretty much felt like I had no choice, but then I'd go out, and there was just too much to think about, and I'd end up coming back in, and finally I thought well let me at least move someplace where I can afford to look out, without the mental overload of actually going out. (Which I do, but maybe not as often as other people. I like to go out on Saturday mornings. I have no problem with that.) Anyway, there was this giant open terrace, overlooking Central Park and the entire city in all directions, and naturally it's semifoggy, and there's a full moon, and maybe Anna's used to it, but even though I live in Chicago now, I'm still a New Yorker, and when you get a view like this, you can't help but feel like it's not even real, like you're in some Woody Allen movie, and I have to tell you, I still love Woody Allen movies, that's probably not politically correct to say anymore, but I do, still, and when I watch those movies with their giant memorabilia-and-art-filled New York apartments I always think, who *are* these people? (Sometimes when Anna and I were in high school we'd get invited to parties by kids of rich and famous people who lived in these duplex and triplex penthouse apartments on Fifth or Park, but [a] we always had a big thing about going to the East Side [the West Side being just better (less snooty more down to earth)], and [b] the parents were never at the parties, so it wasn't like you could get any picture of them in their Woody Allen life, cheating on each other and laughing jovially later among the art books and panoramic city views. Okay, well, Anna did grow up in a kind of giant art-book-filled apartment in a historic landmark building on the West Side, with intellectual parents. But I think they were faithful, and it never seemed so funny.) Then I turned around and Anna opened the door to the solarium, which I'm more inclined to describe as a terrarium, which it seems like it had to have been at some earlier time, filled with greenery and condensation and maybe a turtle, a glass house now occupied by a plain living room set, a table, and a couple of lamps.

It was the exact reverse of my last New York apartment, not just because of its all-window feature but for its sparse decor, which I've never been known for. And it's true, no one was there.

Anna left me alone to write for a while, and I dragged a chair out onto the terrace because it was warm enough and the glass is warped or something inside the solarium. You can totally see out, but everything looks just a little bit wavy. I didn't really get any writing done at all, it was just too much, looking at the stars from up there, and when Anna came back a couple of hours later to check on me, I didn't know I was going to say this, but what came out of my mouth was, *I think I'm just going to sleep up here tonight.* And she, being Anna, said, *Well I'll just go get you a blanket then.* Thoughtful, like I said.

I couldn't really sleep that first night, so I rearranged the furniture in the solarium, mostly just for something to do, but it ended up being kind of unsatisfying because it was all so Swedish plain, and didn't look dramatically different when I was done than it did before I started. Anna came back in the morning and said, *Oh, I like what you've done with the place,* and reminded me that my flight was leaving for Chicago that afternoon, and I said, *Anna, I think I'm just going to stay.* I'm pretty sure she knew what I meant as soon as I said it, but at first she got kind of overexcited because she thought I might possibly have meant that I was going to move back to New York, and when she said, *That's so great!* I finally said, *No, I mean up here.* I think for a second there might have been some mental adjustment she was making, but in a way it worked out well for both of us, since the days are long gone when I could afford to live on the Upper West Side even if I wanted to, and as soon as she figured out that I was serious she said, *Is there anything I can get you?* and I said, *I think I need some wood.*

This might seem like a given, knowing that I grew up in Manhattan, but I didn't have a lot of experience with building, and because I was kind of winging it I figured I'd start with sort of a modest studio, just a bedroom, really, since I already had the whole outside, and the terrarium and everything. (I'm not much of a cook; I've opened my oven about three times since I moved to Chicago, and that was to make toast, which I figure I could pretty well make with, you know, a toaster, which is what Anna had been referring to as my kitchen. She got me a mini-fridge as well.) Anna brought nails and power tools and a ladder, and I looked at it as a sort of biggish game of blocks, but with nails. Believe me, it fell down not a few times before I finally got it right. But I mean, how hard is it really, to nail together a big box? It was just the door and the windows that gave me a little trouble. I made the holes too big, and so you can imagine it was a little drafty at first. But I have to say, when you've finished building a house, of any kind, there's quite a feeling of accomplishment. Someone says, *Hey look at this pot holder I made*, you can say, *Really, well I built this house*.

I left the outside unpainted, for a log-cabiny feel, and Anna helped me choose wallpaper in a tasteful leaf design. She offered to buy me some nice linens, as a sort of housewarming gift, but since she'd already essentially funded the entire project, I told her I thought I could make do with whatever old ones she had around the house. (Strange thing about Anna, she has this beautiful silk bedspread in her room, matching curtains and all, and countless giant fluffy bath sheets, but she's still holding on to numerous ancient shredded towels she tells me have sentimental value, that they belonged to her grandmother. Some of them are worn down to washcloth size. I myself have countless items from long-gone members of the family, but I also think there's a time to let things go, like when it takes you twenty minutes after a shower to get dressed because that's how long it takes to pat yourself dry with what's left of your towel.) She also brought up some extra throw pillows and an afghan for the living room, which helped warm up the place a bit. You know, you can't hang anything up on a glass wall, and obviously you have the skyline and the sky as your art, but still, the decor was just boring.

Anyway, all the home-building and decorating

took a while, and after it was done I wasn't in any rush to leave; still, there wasn't a lot to do. I had thought I might use the opportunity to get some writing done, but if you can believe it, in spite of the view I wasn't terribly inspired. So I didn't see any reason not to have a phone line installed, and by the time I plugged in my modem, there were a lot of e-mails in my box. So I set out to catch up, and when I started to mention to people that I was having this extended stay in New York, when I told them about my deal, a lot of them were pretty envious. I got caught up fairly quickly and continued to keep in touch with people via e-mail or the phone, and of course Anna came up almost every day to hang out, so I really didn't feel lonely at all, in fact, I couldn't think of a more perfect situation. Actually, I had been trying for years to figure out a way to arrange my social life to my exact specifications; I've always had friends, but I never really liked going out, and also I have this thing about being out with large groups of people, together, I mean — if it's more than a single-digit affair, I get kind of overwhelmed and don't know where to direct my attention and something happens inside my head where I start to think that everyone is thinking about me and how odd I look among their double-digit group, and so I avoid certain things altogether, like obviously New Year's Eve has never been a favorite of mine. (The whole idea of New Year's, everyone jumping up and down because this great new year is coming, year after year ignoring the implication that really the next year's going to suck, as evidenced by the fact that these same people will again be, on the following New Year's Eve, jumping up and down because some great new year is coming. If I were the leader of the New Year people, I would institute a more subdued celebration, and perhaps it could be pointed out, on a year-by-year basis, the exact ways in which the past year sucked or didn't suck, and that the celebration could be adjusted accordingly each year. I always wanted to fix it so that I could have, let's say, a New Year's with the exact configuration of my friends that I wanted present, at my house. But people always had other plans by the time I thought of it. Also I get weird about mixing my friends, like I'm responsible for their getting along and having a good time, which is another headache entirely, and another reason I don't entertain.) I don't think this is agoraphobia either, because I knew someone who had agoraphobia, and she had everything delivered and left outside her door so she wouldn't have to see anyone. I like people, I want to see people. I even like meeting new people, I do. I just kind of want it my way.

One day I ordered some lemon chicken from Harriet's Kitchen when Anna wasn't around, and so one of the elevator men brought it up and I was a little concerned at first that he might give me away, but actually not only did he not look surprised at all, I kind of had the feeling he could understand my need for privacy. *Cool,* was pretty much all he said that first time, about my little house, and when he went back down I thought to myself, you know I never really got that whole thing about the UPS guys, but either that elevator costume is working for me or that guy was kinda cute. His hair was short but a little messy, like I like, but mostly it was just the way he had about him. He seemed kind of casual. Like he could see certain things, but maybe they didn't bother him so much. So you can imagine that right away I made a mental note of his schedule, ordered a fuzzy deep lavender sweater from the Internet (it had to be something that I might actually be wearing around the house, so I thought my best bet was to choose an important color, to emphasize my eyes [which are not in fact lavender but a grayish blue that seems to be most blue-looking when set against purple]; this almost ended in embarrassment, because it arrived during his shift and he brought the box up to me himself, but he didn't say anything about it), and a week to the day, called Harriet's for more chicken, two orders. I didn't know what he'd do, but the chicken is just as good the next day, so I wasn't worried about it going to waste. Which it didn't, anyway, because he did stay, only for a little while, because he wasn't really on a break, during which time I of course imagined a lot of testy people waiting for the elevator. He told me he wanted to stay and chat the first time but he thought maybe I didn't want to see anyone. *I don't mind if people come up*, I said. *It's the going out. I'm not very outgoing.* I leaned in to emphasize my little play on words, and he nodded like he understood, but he didn't laugh out loud or anything, and obviously, the guy goes out. *Look, I have to go now*, he said, *but would you mind if I came back another time?*

Let's review: fabulous rent-free Central Park West penthouse, free everything else, cute elevator man wants to come up. This was all working out even better than I'd hoped.

Um, no, not at all, I said.

The elevator man came back the next day; I almost didn't recognize him in his street clothes, black Levi's and a rumply lavender oxford shirt, untucked. I wondered whether to take the lavender as some sign of solidarity. He looked even better than he did in his uniform, but it left me unable to cast him exactly, some cross between edgy and messy prep. He was obviously neither, and although we talked at some length over time, it turned out that he was fully his own person, with some thoughts and ideas I found to be both original and comprehensible. I didn't agree with everything he said, and he didn't seem to need me to, which was sort of a refreshing change from some of my exes, although I can't exactly say whether we were dating or not. Anyway, he told me that his parents were with the circus; I felt it might be invasive to ask in what capacity, but I'm pretty sure they weren't freaks of any kind. He's extremely normal-looking, and also, while he seems to have a sense of humor, he kind of always has this serious look on his face. (You have to look for the twinkle when he's trying to be funny — that's how you can tell, when you're not sure.) They traveled extensively around the country when he was a kid, and then when he was seventeen his parents moved more into circus management and settled down in a small town in Oklahoma, which was about when he moved to New York. He's been an elevator man here in this building almost ever since then.

So you like what you do? I asked.

It's a good job, he said. *It doesn't change much. I like the people. You'd be surprised how interesting that can be.*

I don't think I would, I said. I was thinking how people were often a little too interesting for me. He admitted that he writes a little poetry too. *It's fairly bad,* he said with that twinkle.

Another time he stopped by when I had been looking down onto 73rd Street, trying to figure out about all the people (something I did often, it wasn't any weird coincidence), and I said, *Come here, look,* and he looked and nodded and I said, *Where do they all* go *all the time? Home? Work? Home again?* he asked. *I think so,* I said, *but over and over again like that? I'm pretty sure,* he said, smiling. The elevator man didn't ever ask me a lot of questions, and I'm not stupid, I'm sure my residency on the roof probably answered most of them in his mind. Looking down at all those tiny people moving around like that all the time, home, work, in, out, day after day, I dunno, it just seemed to me like it wasn't me who was acting strange.

A few months went by, and the elevator man and I had gotten to know each other pretty well, and like I said, I was never really sure about the romantic thing, it occurred to me that as much as I knew he liked me as a person maybe he didn't think I was cute or his type or whatever. Maybe his type goes out. Nevertheless, it had been some time since I'd had a real shower (I had running water and a lot of aromatherapy products, that's not my point); there are separate men's and women's bathrooms in the solarium, but no shower, and by then I was longing to have a really good shampoo. So one day I asked the elevator man if he'd mind washing my hair in the sink, and he didn't seem to think this was weird in any way, and the next time he came back with this really nice-smelling chamomile shampoo, which I thought was pretty sweet. We brought a chair into the bathroom, and he put a towel around my neck, and if he were an actual shampooer in some salon, I'd have given him a lot more than two or three dollars, because he was especially careful about getting the temperature just right, and I can't even really describe how great it felt except to say I was just about hallucinating, and he took a lot of time, and I thought about asking him to marry me afterward. The only reason I changed my mind was that we hadn't kissed or anything and I thought it might be too soon. I did ask him if he'd mind doing it once a week, and he said, *Not at all.*

One day Anna came up to tell me that this guy jumped off the roof of one of the other sections of the building, that he was pretty young, married, with a family. She didn't know him at all and there was a little bit of speculation in the building about what the story was; it didn't really matter to me, it was obvious that there was one. Some people said it was money, which seems pretty absurd from my point of view, seeing as how anyone in this building has to be rich, and apparently his health was fine. Other people said it was an accident, but there are very high bars on the terrace, much taller than a very tall person, and so that's pretty unlikely. There wasn't any note. Anna seemed pretty stressed about it, and I guessed that this had never happened to her before, but when I was growing up on West End Avenue, it happened not once but twice in my building, and you know, it's not ever a good thing but it starts to be less of a surprise after the first couple times. The first time we heard a lot of shouting coming from the apartment below us (which was nothing unusual, this forty-year-old guy lived there with his mother, and they were always shouting) and it seemed kind of louder than usual so my dad climbed up on the kitchen sink and looked out the window and there was the guy, hanging halfway out the window threatening to jump, and my dad, lacking any training in any such emergency situations, said, *Get back in there,* to the guy and he actually did, which is totally not what you'd expect, but let me say we were all really glad not to have seen him not get back in there, and a few weeks after that he did jump right out that same window, which thankfully for a lot of the tenants was in the back, and there was no shouting that time. The second time some other person went up to the roof and jumped off the front, right around dinnertime, when my dad was just getting home from work, and my mom and I were both kind of squeamish so we asked him to skip the rest of the grisly details after he told us that they were laying down not one but two white sheets, some distance apart on the sidewalk, to cover up this one person. I walked to and from school smushed up against the building for a while after that.

Anyway, Anna said, *Maybe you should think about coming down.* This was the first time she seemed worried about me at all, all this time, but I assured her, *Anna,* I said, *I'm fine. I'm not going to jump. I'm happy here.* But then the elevator man came up too, to talk about it; I asked him what he thought the story was, he said he didn't ever work in that other section except to cover someone occasionally, but that the one time he saw the guy his impression was that he looked a little sad. I said, *Almost everyone looks sad to me.* The elevator man hadn't seemed concerned about me before either, but he said the same thing Anna did, exactly, *Maybe you should think about coming down.* And I said, *I'm fine, I'm not going to jump,* and he said, *What's the difference, though,* and I said, *What?* and he said again, *What's the difference.* Like a sentence. He said, *It's like you jumped up.*

I didn't really know what to say right then, but a little more time went by, and I have to say I wasn't enjoying my luxury pad so much anymore. I wasn't going to jump. But that thing he said stuck in my head like a burr, like that thing I heard about how A.A. really fucks up your drinking. I never got that before, I kept thinking, *But you're not supposed to drink in*

A.A. But when the elevator man said that thing about jumping up, not only did I have a very visual image of myself in some depressed superhero costume soaring up to the roof, I felt like I couldn't really enjoy my little palace anymore. Plus I was still thinking he was so cute and that there was no chance he was going to want to settle down with me, or up, as he pointed out. A fog rolled in, quickly obliterating the skyline and everything else, and stayed for what seemed like a month; it would've come right into the terrarium if I'd left the door open. The elevator man still came up and hung out and washed my hair, but I was getting to the point where even though my hair felt clean, the rest of me didn't, and I really wanted a shower, and I started having actual dreams about that dinner-plate-size showerhead down at Anna's. Also I thought that the fog would go away sooner or later but it didn't, and apparently I didn't seal up those edges around the door frame so well after all, because the fog eventually crept inside, and after a while I couldn't make out the letters on my keyboard, and then it got so thick I wasn't 100 percent sure I was even there. Finally I found myself tiptoeing into the hallway by the Chihuahuas' place, waiting by the elevator. I didn't hear the Chihuahuas at all, but I didn't know if that was because I was so quiet or if the lawsuit settled in favor of the prosecution. I'm not sure how long I was there, but I hadn't had a chance to ring for the elevator before my elevator man opened the door and let the Chihuahua lady off (no Chihuahuas present, but another dirty look). He smiled at me, the elevator man. *I think I'm just gonna go take a shower at Anna's,* I said.

Cool, said the elevator man.

The Super Fantastic New Zealand Triangle

HER FANTASY IS, at best, unlikely. The man lives in New Zealand. He's married. He has three children. She believes that he is faithful (see: married) and devoted (see: children). She knows that the chance of anything ever happening between them is, as far as anyone is concerned, nonexistent, but recognizes that in a fantasy, the need for any basis in fact is negligible. She does have what is perhaps an unnecessary preoccupation with propriety, given that propriety might not be at the top of one's fantastical concerns. It's not as though the fantasy is going anywhere outside of her head. She's aware that in addition to the impropriety inherent in disclosing the fantasy, even just to the man who the fantasy is about, this particular fantasy might possibly portray her as being somewhat unbalanced. So it's a private, karmically correct, inherently impossible imaginary scenario.

In the fantasy, the man, an actor that the woman has known since she was young and stupid,[1] comes to America after he's cast in a featured role[2] in a Bruce Willis movie that happens to be shooting in Chicago, where she lives.[3] On location there for several weeks with considerable free time, the man and the woman become inseparable[4] and then have to figure out what to do. Finally, the man decides that, on the brink of a major American film career,[5] he will move his family

---

[1] Okay, that might be a little harsh.

[2] As an apprentice criminal whose boyishly innocent appearance masks his true evil

[3] Briefly, the woman considered making the fantasy take place in New Zealand, which is arguably a more beautiful and exotic setting than Chicago, but she's never been there and didn't think she had a lot to say about the atmosphere except for she's heard they have a lot of sheep, finally deciding against it to avoid any sort of sneaking around; even though it's a fantasy, she has a thing about making it as believable as possible, otherwise she has a hard time actually imagining it.

[4] Platonically, but not

[5] A questionable notion; though he's a fine and trained actor, and though the woman thinks he's awfully cute even though he has a lot less hair than he had when they first met, he's more of a character actor than anything else, and the only other reason she can think of why he'd go to the States is if his parents fell ill, or something, and if that ever actually happened later she'd be fairly freaked out at any weird prescience plus having already been through such a thing herself she'd really rather not have some tragedy that isn't even real figure into her fantasy.

back[6] to the States, and the woman will wait to get involved with him until he and his wife drift apart and
eventually get divorced naturally and the wife gives
her blessing to the man and the woman because she
knows they are in true love,[7] and so then the woman
won't have to feel so bad that he lives ten thousand
miles away from his children.[8] The woman won't be
explicit about sex (not her thing, writing about it, because why, why would she do that, why would anyone do that? Sex is the end of something, maybe it's
the end of everything, it matters, but it's not *the* matter; everyone knows it's great, or it should be great,
but it doesn't very often tell you anything in and of
itself, well maybe it does in some very specific circumstances, like if it's really terrible, or if it's violent
[which is certainly not anything this woman has anything to write about] or in some way weird [which
probably she could write about, but still won't], but
she's not interested in that, she thinks there is always
a way to write about whatever is relevant, in any par-

---

[6] Obviously, since the woman has never been to New Zealand, they first
met here, when they were both working at a restaurant in New York.

[7] Likely the most fantastical of concepts in the fantasy

[8] She also thinks that if they did get divorced naturally she could maybe
move to New Zealand, for the sake of the kids, but since her mother died
she feels like she doesn't want to be so far away from her own family,
while they're still around.

ticular sex act, that doesn't require being explicit about the details, that the language available for that subject is fully inadequate, that she rarely reads in a book/sees in a movie a sex scene that's remotely arousing, or that enlightens her in any way,[9] or is more relevant to the piece than some other scene that shows how the two characters interact with each other, certainly she can't even think of one that ever related especially to any of her own experiences, plus her father might read this) but will say that the man is very tender and gentle, but also skilled, and all the way around makes her feel sincerely cared for and truly loved.[10]

That's the fantasy. In reality, the woman has been cheated on and doesn't much care to pass those feelings on to anyone else. She believes that people who cheat once cheat again, although this arguably adds both to his appeal and to the quandary, since he has no history of cheating. He has a history of being faithful. The woman believes in karma. She has a conscience, but it has never really been tested insofar as it's no big

---

[9] Maybe *Lolita*, in which it's totally relevant, but which obviously has no similarity at all here, thank god

[10] Which is the reason she keeps fantasizing about him in particular versus some random movie star, or anyone else she knows who might actually be single and live in the same country; this man is the only one who ever felt this way toward her whose feelings she might also have returned, again, had she not been young and terrified

struggle for her not to steal, or kill, or tell really bad lies, and hasn't fully been tested in this scenario either, because of the New Zealand thing. And, really, she's not even sure how she feels about him. She thinks she could be in love with him. Or that she was in love with him once. That he was the only one she ever loved, really. Or that she could fall in love with him, easily. She thinks he's the one who got away. She remembers all of the romantic gestures[11] and minimizes her previous reservations,[12] the ones she had long before he had a wife, and in some cases doesn't remember the reservations at all.[13] She will deny that this is on her mind for any other reason besides her finally being sober long enough to recognize her feel-

---

[11] Origami birds "because it's Tuesday," daisies "because it's Wednesday," midsummer valentines "because I love you all year" — you get the idea

[12] Basically that he was a crazy lying drug addict, when in fact he was no crazier than her and was not a liar at all, but actually had had a troubled childhood in which certain things occurred that were so unusual and sad that they seemed like lies, but weren't, and furthermore, he gave up drugs about ten years before she gave up booze, which she very much needed to, rest assured, which is to say that she was in no position, really, to be saying anything about anyone's drug problems

[13] For example she has no recollection at all about being completely and totally overwhelmed by the intensity of his feelings for her, which had a lot more to do with why she never even kissed him, if you can fucking believe that, than his being a crazy lying drug addict (which didn't prevent her from subsequently getting involved with a long list of psychos/liars/drug addicts who were not in any way as intensely in love with her as the man was).

ings, past and present. In reality she has seen him once, seven years ago,[14] and the time before was probably seven years prior to that.[15] Mostly, this is about

---

[14] On a trip to L.A., where he lived at the time, they had breakfast at Hugo's, which is as close to an actual date as they ever had (when you think about it, when they were kids they didn't have any money and tended to just walk around all the time) even though he was already married then, and even though they still never kissed but by then they were talking about it, or more accurately now he's not the only one talking about it, and when he tells her that someday he's going to just have to kiss her, someday when he makes his wife understand that this started long ago and it has nothing to do with her and that she should just understand it as retroactive, or something, and when he tells the woman that he wants to kiss her, she says okay instead of saying don't say that or stop it or something; there were discussions that involved flirting/negotiations of possible kissing in which they both participated.

[15] In a dark railroad apartment (which the woman has never been especially fond of, she likes walls and doors [and does not very much like lofts for the same reason] and also it was on the Upper East Side, *way* Upper, a little scary, and probably at least subliminally confirming her earlier reservations) where he was by then living with the woman who would become his wife, who the woman met only that one time for about a minute and so therefore has no particular opinion about (although as a rule, she does have a habit of thinking the women who replace her are either genius supermodels [in which case it's easy for her to say, well of course, I can't compete with that] or genius scullery maids [in which case she can feel better about herself (and yet simultaneously worse, knowing that the man has chosen the genius scullery maid on the basis of something other than her appearance) although the truth is that this isn't an entirely relevant point, considering that the genius/supermodel/scullery maid quandary tends to pertain more to situations in which she's been rejected and in this case it *is* very relevant that she was not, and yet, her mind is inclined to go to the g/s/s.m. place anyway, just in case it enlightens her as to any possible means to self-improvement, some way to be more genius supermodel scullery maid-like, which anyone ought to know is probably the wrong way to go

something that was unresolved for a couple of summers in New York when she was home from college[16] and a few love letters[17] and moony long-distance phone calls.[18] This is about a kiss that never happened.

---

about self-improvement, not to mention that it's toward a questionable end anyway] which maybe gets into an issue she has that possibly has nothing to do with reality, or has to do with the choices she's making and not the supermodel-chooser, but if you think about it, either way she's lost). This visit falls into a period of some years before she quit drinking where she had stopped thinking about him as a romantic question mark, stopped thinking about him at all for a while, stopped thinking about much of anything.

[16] Trying not to drink so much while also trying to forget that the English department at her school really sucked and that the guys she went to school with were a bunch of gold jewelry–wearing, nose-jobbed, perm-headed (seriously), Sergio Valente/whistle-around-their-neck, disco-dancing, coke-sniffing, put-their-dick-in-fucking-anything-that-paused fucking stupid greedy fucked-up motherfucking assholes

[17] One card had a picture of a naked boy and girl and the girl is kind of innocently touching the boy, which at the time the woman thought was provocative and shocking and which is now pinned to her bulletin board.

[18] There was that one time he called at her father's house in Iowa, only she hadn't given him the number there and it was kind of late, even though everyone in the house was still up (this was another reservation she maybe didn't so much forget but maybe she doesn't see it as so upsetting now as it seemed then, all she remembers thinking is, *It's ten-thirty! Ten-thirty!* but now that she's remembering it better it might have been more about him telling her he missed her and loved her loved every single hair on her head loved the way she laughed loved the way she looked at him *what are you talking about I don't look at you like anything* that freaked out her teenage self than it being ten-thirty, you know, when everyone was going to sit down and watch Carson anyway).

Now, they talk[19] or exchange a card or letter about once or twice a year. Now, he has three kids, lives in New Zealand, has a good career and apparently it's very beautiful and affordable there and he would have no good reason to leave and six good reasons to stay. Or, in the event that any part of the fantasy ever came true, one reason to think about leaving and five much better reasons to stay. Or one person to try to

---

[19] He called her the first few times after he moved to New Zealand (or, he returned her calls, the point is it was his dime, or maybe there are two points [the truth is it's entirely possible that the tables have totally turned, or that they've turned part of the way around, at least, given that after she rejected him in the first place, he eventually got over it, enough to marry and have kids and move out of the country anyway, and even though when they talk he says he loves her and it's like they're back in time except she's not totally freaked out and even though she thinks people don't/shouldn't say things like that if they're (supposedly) happily married, she would probably, if backed against a wall, admit that she's the one to keep in touch with him more than the other way around, even though he obviously likes it, and it may be that it is a lot easier for him, under the day-to-day circumstances of raising a family and all, in New Zealand, 8,187 miles from Chicago, to be aware of the severe unlikelihood of this particular tragic romance ever coming to fruition]) and then one time she called him and that one call cost $117, so now she either writes or actually what she does is she writes and then tears up the letters because even that seems really wrong, and then she writes letters that are just stiff and boring, like about the weather, and work or whatever, she just sewed curtains, which every time he calls he calls her on and says *why are you telling me about curtains,* and he's right, except when it gets onto paper what she's only been thinking or talking about seems more real and wrong than just saying things into the universe, to disperse, even if it's just him who ends up saying things like he always used to say when it wasn't against

convince to move to New Zealand and no reason to leave. Now, she has a bookmark on her Internet service that tells her what time it is in New Zealand (she can never remember if it's thirteen or seventeen hours ahead, but whenever they talk it's usually the next day there; whichever it is, the day that she's in is usually done for him [and she's not even going to think about that metaphor]) and checks it whenever she's thinking about calling him, which of course is almost always in the middle of the night, or at the crack of dawn, which again, points to the severely poor chances between them, considering there's only maybe a half hour of the day when they're both awake, in their separate hemispheres. Now, although she certainly has a much better life than she ever had

---

the Commandments, she feels like she's somehow more blameless if she lets him say the things, like she's some cerebral fucking female Bill Clinton, which is obviously a bunch of fucking bullshit, and so in the end, especially whenever it seems like there actually is a possibility of them ever seeing each other in person again, she freaks out and feels terrible and so just fantasizes about him but secretly though, she thinks about asking him, just to know, just to find out if he *would*, if he would ever just get on a plane and come to see her, and she thinks he would, if she really wanted him to, which is obviously bad, because either way, either way it goes, either she finds out that when they are finally face-to-face for a week or two or a day or whatever, finds out that he taps his fingers repeatedly like people do, or wears really bad shoes or Dockers or something, or that he listens to 'NSync, or that she still, twenty years later, can't deal with a person who is sincerely, truly in love with her, or she can, she can deal, and she's an adulterer.

before, doing work she wants to do and growing flowers and living in a city that feels like home and no
longer feeling completely confused, or stressed out, or
worried, or frustrated, or not useful, or not appreci-
ated, not most of the time anyway, she does have a little bit more time than she has in the past, a little too
much time, to contemplate her love life, which even
though it has not gotten worse, recently, has not im-
proved and has actually kind of dematerialized altogether. But anyway, he does still say sweet romantic
things like he used to and keeps telling her he loves
her in that shy kind of way that totally breaks her
heart and eventually it comes out that he was in fact
separated for almost a year, which she didn't hear
about until it was over, and apparently it wasn't because either of them was unfaithful, although he
makes it out like it was more his fault than hers, except he doesn't really say in what way, but which
makes it seem like they really did drift apart naturally. The woman asks him why he didn't call her that
whole time, and he says, *Are you joking? If I had
talked to you even once I would have been on a plane
to the States in a second and never looked back.*
Meaning, you know, good for her, and bad for the
three kids and the wife. Which makes it even more
tragic a tale of heartbreak, when you think about the
lengths she goes to to set up a fantasy in which she's

not a totally terrible person, when it turns out there was a whole year when she wouldn't have been any kind of a terrible person if the super fantasy had been real.

But it probably doesn't matter.
Because it will not happen this way.

You Take Naps

HE IS TOO YOUNG.

You are Mrs. Robinson and Gloria Vanderbilt and Cher in the bagel-boy phase and that other singer who's about eighty and in a wheelchair and has a thirty-year-old "beau" is what she calls him. Martha Raye.

You are robbing the cradle.

You look young for your age, but so does he. He looks like he's in high school. You would look old in grad school.

You have many common interests.

You have several common interests.

You have at least one significant interest in common that provides many hours of conversation.

You have nothing in common.

Over dinner, he says smart things. He seems interested in your opinion about smart things. You think, *He's so smart. He's so smart and cute and nice. When he was born, you were a high school freshman. When he was born, you were a high school freshman.* You think this twice. You think, *When you were getting kissed for the first time, he was* crawling. You follow this thought process through a few more developmental stages. You wonder when his birthday is. If his birthday is soon, you might only be 13½ years older than him. If his birthday is not soon, you could be as much as 14¾ years older than him. You realize you have not measured age in quarter-years since you were eleven. You wonder if this thought means anything, if this thought possibly averages your mental age closer to his real age. You notice that he is still talking. You check back in to what he's saying about some philosopher you've never read and you think, *I don't even understand philosophy he's smarter than I am I am a terrible harsh judgmental ageist.*

He has roommates.

You have furniture. You put photos in frames. You have a TV schedule. You have seen *The Brady Bunch* in prime time.

He goes out. He is schedule-free. He is spontaneous. You take naps.

He talks to strangers.

You are from New York.

He has a tendency to be late.

You have a tendency to be there before it opens.

He thinks five hundred dollars is a lot of money.

You think five hundred dollars is a beaded hand-bag with a picture of a pug embroidered on it.

He says *Wow* a lot when you tell your stories. You wonder if this is because he doesn't have that many stories yet or because he's from the suburbs. You wonder why none of those stories seemed *Wow* to you at the time. You frankly wish for a little less *Wow*. He's likely to seek it out.

He worries about things.

You used to worry about things. You stopped worrying about things a few years ago when you finally figured out that both marvelous and tragic things happened whether or not you worried about them. When he tells you his worries you suppress an instinct to use phrases that begin with *When I was your age* or *Oh, honey*. When he tells you his parents are driving him crazy you suppress both those phrases as well as any information about how dealing with one's parents gets simultaneously better and worse as time goes by.

He kisses you sweetly, but you would believe it if you found out it was his first time.

You swear you will not sleep at his house.

You sleep at his house. With makeup on. You have

not gone to bed with your makeup on since you quit drinking. You get up to leave early. You try not to be seen at that hour with your actual face, but he walks you to the door.

You have experience.

He has hope.

You have hope too.

But you hate a cheesy ending. So you amend that; You have hope too, but maybe not for the same things. You want the ending to be neither cheesy nor gloomy. You want the ending to be open. You want an open ending. You want an open, hopeful ending whether it involves you being with the young man, or not being with the young man. An ending where, at the very least, the young man walks away having discovered the ~~rejuvenating~~ revitalizing benefits of the afternoon nap. An ending where it's more likely that you and/or the young man learned something useful and/or possibly had a great love affair than an ending where no learning took place or that a learning of a bitter nature took place where one or both of you made note that there are no great love affairs and that even couples born on the same day of the same year who think they're in love are kidding themselves. You want an ending of hope tempered only in the slightest way by experience. You want an ending of cautious hope.

Better.

Josie and Hyman Differ in Their Use of the Word *Fuck*

SCHOOL IS TAKING a little longer than expected.

Most of her friends have graduated, so she spends a lot of weekends in New York. She doesn't want to be where she is. Her salary from the bank (she knows nothing about banking; she answers the phones) affords her a ticket on the Metroliner every other weekend. It doesn't occur to her to save it. Josie is not thinking that far ahead.

She has a *fucking buddy* (she doesn't much like that term but likes *lover* even less especially when there's not much love) from the senior class who sometimes comes over on weekends when she hangs around Philly, but although he's good at getting the job done well and quickly, lately he's gotten into a thing where he likes to watch her, and she doesn't much like putting on a show. She figures that she doesn't need anyone else in the room who isn't going to participate. She doesn't really care about watching him.

Josie has a friend in New York named Nadine. Josie and Nadine went to high school together. Nadine is an actress. Josie doesn't want to be an actress, but she wouldn't mind being Nadine. Nadine has excellent posture. Nadine's posture, Josie thinks, explains everything you need to know about Nadine. Her grammar is good and her diction is better. She does not leave syllables unpronounced. She does not use slang. Nadine has all kinds of men making her all kinds of offers at all times. On a New York weekend, Josie meets Nadine for a $6.98 all-you-can-drink champagne brunch at an East Side restaurant called the Racing Club. Nadine brings a pair of excess suitors with her, Hyman and Hayes. Those are their real names.

Hayes works for a bank, a Wall Street bank. Hayes knows something about banking. Hayes thinks he has something in common with Josie because of the bank thing, but he really doesn't. Hyman is a composer. Hyman lives in *Boston and New York*. Hyman and Josie probably do have a few things in common, but Hyman could kind of care less. Hyman thinks Josie is *beautiful*. It is apparent that Hayes thinks Josie is beautiful too, but Hayes has *nice guy* written all over his seersucker jacket. Hyman is *interesting*. Hyman wears horn-rimmed glasses.

Nadine's posture aside, the attention of Hyman and Hayes is mostly fixed on Josie. Hyman dominates the conversation some, asks Josie a lot of questions. Josie doesn't ask a lot of questions of anyone, but Hyman finds a way to mention that he went to Yale and got near-perfect SAT scores. It seems that in spite of an 800 on math, Hyman scored only a 780 on verbal, something he prides himself on, his verbal skills, and has, approximately nine years after having taken the SATs, never really gotten over it. Josie has been called an underachiever. Josie has never stopped to break down that word, or to look it up. She doesn't understand that it means she can do better. She accepts that it means she can't.

Hyman tells a story involving a menorah and begins to explain to Josie what a menorah is. Josie is not Jewish but takes this kind of personally. *For god's sake, Hyman*, Nadine says, *she's been to my house for Hanukkah. She's from New York.* Hayes, also from New York, says, *I'd like to know what a menorah is*, and everyone laughs except for Hayes. Hyman says, *Maybe you'd like to explain, Josie*, in a playfully challenging tone and Josie says to Hayes, *It's sort of a candelabra with nine candles that represent the creation.*

Sometimes seven, Hyman says. Nadine says, *Oh Hyman stop it already.* Later in the conversation Hyman tries to explain a few more things Josie already knows. Hyman touches her arm and tries to feed her cake and makes double entendres about having a three-way with Nadine and Josie and throws a couple of blatant insults over to Hayes, mostly regarding his seersucker jacket and his full-size umbrella that keeps falling off the side of the table onto the floor. The umbrella insults have to do with it being sunny. Josie has six mimosas and hardly catches a buzz and Hayes politely asks for her number after lunch. Hyman pulls Josie over and whispers loudly, *Give him the wrong number.*

Nadine calls Josie to report that *the gentlemen were enraptured,* and that she gave Hayes her address and Hyman her numbers in New York and Philly. Hyman calls at the crack of dawn the next morning, before her train back to school, asking her out for a date the next time she comes to New York. Josie picks up a copy of *People* magazine at Penn Station and discovers an article about Hyman's mother, an actress who had been famous in the sixties and then kind of disappeared and later wrote a tell-all book about her subsequent life as a Turkish porn star. Naturally, Josie runs out to buy the book, which she reads with a certain amount of guilt. She feels like she's cheating. She realizes she is going to have moments when Hyman is going to tell her things that she already knows and that she is going to lie. She does not realize that she probably started lying to Hyman before brunch was over. Josie finishes the book in one evening and identifies with Hyman's mother on account of her being in love with a brilliant film director to whom she feels intellectually inferior. Josie isn't really sure if Hyman's mother feels less inferior at the end of the book or not, it seems like she just feels glad not to be a Turkish porn star anymore.

Josie receives a letter from Hayes two days after her return to Philly, a letter that says things like *it was very nice to meet you* and *I would be honored if you would agree to dine with me when you return to New York.* Josie does not feel attracted to Hayes, but feels that she should. A few days later Hayes calls Josie *to follow up the letter* and Josie agrees to meet him for lunch but feels like telling him to bring a résumé. Josie wishes that Hyman would call her in Philly to use words like *honor,* but he does not call until she gets back to New York, at which time he invites her to an opera opening, an opening of an *innovative* production of *Carmen.* Hyman takes some time to explain about the innovation and about opera in general before Josie, the daughter of a soprano, who has seen quite a few operas in her short life, who has seen quite a few performances of *Carmen,* politely says, *Yes I know the story of* Carmen, without any additional information that would possibly convey to Hyman that she knows anything at all. She does not want to be seen as pretentious. She does not want to seem like Hyman. In fact Hyman is certainly not thinking Josie is pretentious. Hyman is thinking about what he can *contribute*. Josie says she has to go and is a little bit late to meet Hayes, who has been waiting at the restaurant for twenty-five minutes even though Josie is really only about seven minutes late. Hayes is holding a single rose.

Josie does not normally have two dates in one day. Men like her, but her experience is such that more than one date per day can be confusing. Plus, she just doesn't like that many guys. So it doesn't often come up. Josie feels a little guilty about having lunch with Hayes knowing that she likes Hyman. Hayes asks Josie a few questions about the bank but Josie doesn't have much to say about it that's interesting to her except that the guys in accounting stumble in hungover a lot. Hayes is looking more for an interest in finance. Josie says her interest in finance is limited to having a little. Hayes laughs very loudly, a *ho ho ho* kind of fakey laugh. Josie blurts out that she's not looking for anything serious right now and just wants to concentrate on *graduating and getting a good job,* which isn't true. Josie wants to concentrate on Hyman. Hayes says he understands but looks like he doesn't, asks if he can write her again. Josie says sure.

Josie picks out a black angora sweater and a long skirt to wear to the opera. Hyman, in rumpled corduroys, takes her out for Thai food for dinner. She has never had Thai food before, not even on a long layover in the Bangkok airport. Again, she leaves out the Bangkok information which might possibly lead to some world-traveling/informed sort of conversation, which Josie is more capable of than she realizes, accepting her underachievement, and Hyman orders a variety of dishes for them to share, happy to educate. Josie has had just about all the education she feels she needs, what with the ninth semester she's finishing up now, and would just as soon sample the Thai food and then decide whether or not she likes Thai food without so much education, but overall she is highly impressed that Hyman is so intelligent and especially how that reflects on her. Josie and Hyman share the usual bit of first-date family history and Josie enjoys that his family (divorce, actors, pornography) is even more exotic than hers (divorce, musicians, manic depression). Hyman wastes no time mentioning his mother's recent tell-all with unhesitating disdain. Josie pretends she had no idea about the book but asks why it bothers him. Hyman says, *It's just so sordid.* Left out of the tell-all was the information that in high school, Hyman's mother, in an effort to help Hyman become a man (due to an unusually large head, which he claims only to have *grown into* later, a questionable occurrence) at the late age of sixteen, arranged for him to be deflowered by one of her Turkish colleagues. Josie doesn't really know what to say about this but she's thinking maybe Hyman lost those twenty SAT points on the definition of *sordid*. Hyman mentions over spring rolls that when they lived in Turkey there was no TV and that there wasn't anything to do but read or fuck, and *There was only so much reading, ha.* Josie says, *No TV?* and wonders aloud how she'd ever live without *Days of Our Lives* and Hyman grimaces and says, *Oh you didn't just say that!* clutching his heart as though he has just been stabbed and says television is *odious* and that he would never allow his children to be *brainwashed by our spurious culture.* Josie writes off ever having kids with Hyman but says nothing and they walk to Lincoln Center after dinner and Josie explains her theory of happiness and weather, how if a person can be happy in the winter then they must be truly happy in spite of gray, gloomy weather, that in the summer you might not know if you're naturally happy because it's easy to be cheerful on a beautiful day. Hyman laughs and puts his arm around her. *You are wonderful,* he says. Hyman kisses her before they even get to *Carmen* and asks her to be his date for a wedding he *doesn't approve of* the following weekend in Philly. Josie agrees to the date but asks him about the disapproval and Hyman says they're just *not on the same level. What level is that,* Josie asks, and Hyman says, *An intellectual level.* Josie says, *Is that next to ladies lingerie?* and Hyman says, *Clever,* and gives Josie a squeeze but doesn't laugh.

Hyman comes to Philly for the date wearing an Armani suit, which impresses Josie but seems uncharacteristic given his disdain for all things bourgeois, until they take the train to the wedding in Cherry Hill. Hyman introduces Josie to the couple at the reception as his *friend* but proceeds to try to make out with her over dessert, which public display of affection has never been her thing even under the influence of limitless free champagne. Josie tries to join the conversation with the intellectual/nonintellectual bride and groom but remains largely without comment. During a long and heated discussion about race relations during which Josie mostly remains silent (at one point, referring to the participants in the discussion/everyone present at the wedding being very very white, she says, *What do any of us really know about race relations?* to which Hyman says, *You're so cute* and kisses her on the head). Josie's uncertainty about which one of the newlyweds is on the lower level of intellect serves only to suggest that this particular uncertainty is not going to work in her favor with Hyman long-term. Hyman tries to sleep over at Josie's apartment and Josie says, *Not this time.* Josie doesn't have any particular rules about when she sleeps with someone but after only two dates is feeling uncertain that Hyman is interested in anything other than sex as a goal, and Josie has other goals in mind. Josie has graduation coming up.

She skips the ceremony. Graduating in December with the other underachievers seems anticlimactic to her. She will put in her forwarding address and wait to receive her *communications degree* in the mail. Josie just wants to go home. She does not yet realize that living in a two-bedroom apartment on the Upper West Side with a manic-depressive opera singer and her husband may not be the best environment for her to begin her new life. Things go all right for a while. The opera singer and the husband are figuring that Josie will move out as soon as she gets a job. Josie is figuring that she will move out in about a year after she's saved a little money. It will be about a month before all involved realize that they are not figuring on the same things.

Hyman, over the course of eight days, gives Josie a series of increasingly odd Hanukkah presents. Josie is not expecting presents and wouldn't have the first idea what to buy someone after two dates anyway. On the first day he gives her dark chocolate Hanukkah gelt. Josie is impressed by the fact that he's found dark chocolate Hanukkah gelt until he comments that *dark chocolate is just better*, which seems, in spite of being an opinion Josie shares, too definitive. Someone in the world, she thinks, likes milk better. On the second day he gives her a miniature cactus and on the third day he gives her a packet of multivitamins. On the fourth day he gives her a pair of earrings shaped like tiny telephones and explains his feeling that now that she's moving back to New York she needs to have some *style*. Josie will never wear these earrings, not even just to please Hyman. But she will wear the socks he gives her on the fifth day, the socks with tiny terriers on them (they won't show much under her jeans), and she will wear the stockings he gives her on the sixth day, the stockings with the Chinese pattern on them (they won't show much under a long skirt, although Hyman will tell her *they're meant to go with a mini*), but she will not wear the fishnets Hyman gives her on the seventh day, not even *in private* as Hyman is hoping, and she will definitely not wear the rhinestone "Boy Toy" belt he gives her on the eighth day, not even/especially when provided with the argument that *Madonna gets the joke*. Madonna probably does, but Josie thinks she's not so sure about Hyman.

New Year's Eve is spent riding around in a limousine going to parties at the apartments of aging movie stars with Hyman and his father and his father's French model/Ph.D.-candidate girlfriend of approximately the same age as Josie but with a well-developed indifference. At three in the morning the couples return to Hyman's father's apartment for a bottle of Cristal and to listen to a recording of Hyman's new *piece*, a piece Hyman has spent the last three years on, twenty-three excruciating minutes of some kind of vaguely musical collage (bits and pieces from existing operas, subway trains, screams, and blaxploitation films) entitled "Red Vines, Jerky and String Cheese, a fugue" (provoking a loud *Hoo Hoo! Oh, perfection!* from Hyman's father and a smirk from his girlfrend). Josie, from a musical household/Manhattan, is more than familiar with classical music as well as with noise and is certain that this *piece* far more closely resembles the latter, is certain that she could not have lived through this *piece* if it were twenty-four minutes long, endures the *piece* silently to the continued guffaws from Hyman's father, to the nods of understanding from the French girlfriend, with only a blank stare on her own part, in this case unbeknownst to Hyman, because it is all she can do to conceal her utter hatred of this pretentious near–half hour of garbage, only to suffer through the *piece* once again after cries of *Brilliant!* from Hyman's father and once again after that to *catch all the nuances*. Josie can think of no more painful way to spend sixty-nine minutes of her life (plus commentary) and is grateful only that the Cristal continues to flow. Hyman tries to fool around with Josie in the limo on the way back to her apartment, but it's only eight blocks away and the Cristal/*piece* have eliminated any desire.

Josie meets Nadine for a New Year's Day champagne brunch on the East Side. *Hayes begged me to let him come,* Nadine says with a guilty laugh. *But I hear someone else is smitten with you as well. I don't know, Nadine,* Josie says. *I don't think I'm smart enough for him.* Nadine rolls her eyes and says, *Please! Hyman's a dear friend but someone needs to shove those SAT scores up his ass already. You can't be taking that intellectual nonsense seriously.* Josie admits that she is and explains about the *piece* and says, *There isn't enough champagne on the entire West Side to make that tolerable.* Nadine groans and says, *Well we're on the East Side now, darling,* and orders another round of mimosas. *I'm going to call that bonehead up and tell him to move to the back of the line!* Josie says, *It's a short line,* and in dispute Nadine points out a cluster of cute waiters looking her way and tells Josie she's as bright as anyone she knows and that if Hyman doesn't see that he's a *fool.* Josie always feels a little stronger after champagne with Nadine in the morning.

Josie goes on a job interview for a network news station and, fairly certain that she will get the job, goes to visit Hyman for the weekend in Boston, where he teaches music. Josie asks how cold it is there and he tells her not to worry about it, that if he can help it they'll be spending the weekend indoors. Josie and Hyman still haven't had sex, but they have been doing a lot of other stuff. Josie and Hyman do spend some time out of doors, and it is cold, and Josie eventually decides that they should spend the rest of the weekend indoors, even if it means consenting to the sex, because Hyman wears a terrible navy blue polyester knit hat, a hat that Josie thinks does not reflect any sense of *style*, a hat that he left in the last taxi and which hat, a hat seen on the seat after Hyman's exit from the taxi, a blue polyester knit hat that Josie thought better of retrieving, to no avail because it was replaced the following day with a red polyester knit hat for $3.99 in front of Tower Records. Hyman says, *I lose a lot of hats.* Josie thinks, *Not enough.*

Josie and Hyman have sex. Hyman refers to sex as *fucking.* Josie, who would not refer to sex as anything but sex, would not call it making love even if she were madly in love, due to what she sees as an utter lack of meaning (Josie feels strongly that if you're going to use the word *make* in this scenario you should also use the word *baby*, because that is the only possible thing that could be made from that particular act besides maybe a mess, and even Josie would have to agree that neither *let's make a mess* nor *let's make a baby*, in this particular case, would be a turn-on). Shortly after Josie and Hyman have sex, postsex, mid-Hyman talking about sex, *That was a great fuck* or some such, Josie lies in Hyman's bed wondering if this is supposed to be arousing, if this sort of talk is arousing to people, if this sort of talk is expected in return. Josie says the word *fuck* often enough, but prefers it followed by *off* or *up*, or as an adverb, or even isolated by itself in moments of frustration. Josie is listening to the postsex wrap-up, to Hyman's allegedly seductive description of her body parts, trying to think of anything at all to contribute, when *her mother calls*. Josie's mother is upset. Josie has gotten a call from the network regarding her social security number and Josie's mother says, *People have no business going out of town when they're supposed to be trying to get a job,* and then she says, *Are you having a good time? What have you been doing?* in a completely sweet tone of voice that bears no resemblance to her initial comment and Josie says, *I'll call you back later,* and gets off the phone. Josie has a hard time concealing her embarrassment and Hyman, in a surprising turn of sensitivity, offers as consolation a story about a time when he was in bed with a *lover* in New York and his father called to remind him to water the plants.

Josie returns to New York and starts her job at the network. She is assigned to the traffic department, which she is to learn is not about actual traffic, where she will be an assistant. She is assigned to the overnight shift. She will work one to nine. She will pay her dues. Josie does not anticipate how this will actually affect her. Josie will come to understand and appreciate manic depression. Trying to sleep during daylight hours in a two-bedroom apartment with an unmedicated manic-depressive opera singer and her husband will give Josie a certain appreciation for the breaking down of normal mental functions. After five days of working the one-to-nine shift Josie will take short breaks to cry in the bathroom, after eight days of working the one-to-nine shift Josie will cry for a good portion of any time not spent sleeping, and after ten days of working the one-to-nine shift Josie will turn in her resignation with a plan to enroll in the International Bartenders School.

Josie's mother says, *Well, that was hasty. Because we were hoping you'd have found your own place by now. Look at your cute doggie socks!* None of this is helped by Hyman's presence in town for the debut of his *piece* at City Center. Josie welcomes the distraction in spite of his repeated requests for a fuck, which she obliges without ever voicing her objection to this particular use of the word. Josie tells her mother she's got a lot of job interviews and instead spends a lot of time with Hyman during the day. Hyman loves an afternoon fuck anyway and admonishes Josie for the deception but admits to getting an additional thrill from foiling the plans of anyone's mother. Josie and Hyman spend the afternoon of February the 14th at the Guggenheim Museum on which day the only mention made of St. Valentine's Day is a sideways glance and a mumble of *foolish American contrivance* from Hyman to a woman blissfully carrying a bouquet of daisies in one hand, an adoring date in the other, and a satisfied look in her eye, a February 14 wherein they move up the Guggenheim's spiral at a snail's pace, Hyman lingering at each painting for what seems to Josie like an hour to describe *juxtapositions of color and light and balance* and whatever else endlessly to the point where Josie is forced, after only one rotation around the spiral, into blurting out, *Do you like it?*, which direct question neither gets answered nor makes what she thought was a fairly obvious point, which question results only in Hyman stroking Josie's hair with deceptive affection, suggesting a more sophisticated haircut *now that she's out of college* and requesting an afternoon fuck, possibly somewhere in Central Park. Josie says, *Maybe tomorrow.* Josie is tired of the word *fuck* now. Josie returns home to a valentine from Hayes made from the *Wall Street Journal* and a lot of red glitter. Josie is no more interested in Hayes than she ever was, but she is a little less interested in Hyman.

Josie and Hyman meet at Café La Fortuna for cappuccino the following afternoon. Hyman wastes no time reaching under the table and in between Josie's legs. *Hyman,* Josie says, pushing his hand away, not smiling, as Hyman is, *I want to talk about where this is going.* Hyman says, *Okay well then let's have a big discussion then, ha ha.* Josie can't even begin to guess what is funny to Hyman in this moment but when he sees that Josie is not also laughing he mentions his SAT scores yet again in evidence of the fact that they are very different, that he is four years older than she is and therefore he *will always be ahead* of her and furthermore that she clearly has *unresolved issues with her mother* that she will have to work out before she has a *real relationship* with *anyone* but that he *truly enjoys* her company and was hoping that they could *continue fucking* for an *indefinite period of time* as he *likes fucking her very much.* Josie, who has an opening to hurl a great variety of insults at Hyman regarding his own mother and father and regarding his obsession with his SAT scores, instead calmly stands up and says, *But I don't fucking like* you *very much,* which is the best she can do under the circumstances, which even Josie knows is the kind of response that in seventh grade would have provoked the sarcastic *Nice comeback* in return, and which of course produces loud guffaws from Hyman as Josie leaves the restaurant without saying good-bye. Several years and a few more appreciative boyfriends later, Josie plans to tell Hyman, if she ever sees him again, that he was an *elitist fuck*, but when the time comes and Josie runs into Hyman on the street, even after he says, *I see you still have the same haircut*, Josie still can't bring herself to say anything rude but keeps the plan open for another time.

Year-at-a-Glance

WHEN MY DAD comes to me with the all-purpose serious tone that turns up in a variety of scenarios ranging from me forgetting to pick up milk to him forgetting to get me the concert tickets I asked for to car accidents varying in degree from chipped paint to fender-bender, I naturally fail to understand, upon hearing the words *cancer* and *lung* and *mom* in the same sentence, that it may not turn out well. Which is followed by me spending the next two years failing to understand that. And so of course, when the doctors tell us that she's expected to have a full recovery, this is then followed by me believing them, followed by me moving out of town as proof of my faith in the medical community. Subsequent things that will help me not to understand this:

- my mother saying *I'm fine* and demonstrating this by renting a U-Haul and driving me and everything I own from New Jersey to Chicago
- my mother reupholstering the sofa
- my mother retiling the bathroom
- my mother performing in Mahler's Eighth and receiving rave reviews

(My mother is already an opera singer, so it's not like the old doctor-will-I-ever-play-the-piano kind of situation, still, someone with a lung problem singing, you know, opera, is not only impressive but is a fine tool for furthering denial.)

Several combinations of chemo and radiation and new age crap later, when the doctors say that if this round doesn't work she might only have a few months, I begin a six-hour crying jag that turns my face into a pomegranate and results in the sensation of having a big wad of bubblegum burst inside my skull, which is followed by me wiping away my tears and realizing that the doctors must be completely wrong. I fly back to New York to see her more often even though the city makes me want to slash my wrists and even though I think I won't live through one more person pressing up against me on the subway and even though my mother is even more mood-oriented than before the cancer/lung thing. As a show of my faith in her ability to function as usual, I let my mother drive to Taco Bell (when she sends me back into the house to retrieve her *book* — a tattered Week-at-a-Glance calendar/address combo crammed with assorted scraps of paper, napkins, unpaid bills, to-do lists, fabric swatches, and bus tickets, held together by the combined strength of a rubber band and a size 10 clamp — the opportunity for better judgment arises and is ultimately rejected upon returning to the car and witnessing the first glimmer of hope I've seen in my mother's eyes in months). This even though Mom was more than a little stressed out as a driver before she was attached to an oxygen tank and on prednisone and Xanax and antibiotics and whatever else and because she wants a chicken taco *really bad* and because driving makes her feel like she has some control over her life which we both know she doesn't now, if she ever did, and because I can't decide which frightens me more, me driving at all with her in the passenger seat (*what if she tries to have a conversation while I'm driving what if I drive too fast or slow what if she tells me to make a left turn but there's no left turn signal what if I have a terrible accident and kill my dying mother what if I have a terrible accident and something worse than death happens to my dying mother what if she yells at me?*) or her driving on drugs. Which is followed by me agreeing to continue on the trip *just a little ways* (in reality three interminable highway exits during which she flips off a truck driver and honks at an old lady [not any kind of change from her normal driving patterns] and misses the exit [to which she says, *Whoops!* and giggles even though I know that this spacey part of the tour is the abnormal part]) to the fabric and crafts store to pick up some yarn for a needlepoint she's making for my cousin's new baby. This of course is followed by a variety of thought patterns, like how I'm thirty-six and still single and she's not going to be making any needlepoint anything for my baby, like how I've failed as a daughter, like how I might have considered this a lot sooner, how surely if I'd gone to medical school or taught children in Third World countries or written an Oprah book or achieved some other phenomenal thing she'd have been proud of me in spite of my not having given her a grandchild and a son-in-law or even a live-in boyfriend or lesbian life partner. All of which I actually did consider sooner, which clearly indicates my true nature as a selfish, horrible child. I try to pretend I don't notice the weird tone after I compliment her new car and she responds by saying, *Glad to hear* that, in which I sense she's glad to hear that because it's about to be mine. I tell her I'd really rather skip the Pre-Season Ornament Extravaganza at Fountains of Wayne but decide not to mention that it's because I'm afraid she won't be here when the actual season comes around.

That said, I believe the doctor when he says the unpronounceable drugs are working and that my mother is showing great improvement. I am nonchalant helping her look through brochures for those stairway elevator-seat things and I sob underneath my pillow when I go to bed, grateful that the noisy oxygen machine is probably drowning me out anyway. I tell her all the things I'm grateful for that she's done for me and I do not take it personally when she says only, *That's nice, sweetheart,* and then falls asleep in the middle of my long list instead of bursting into tears of gratitude herself followed by a deep and profound TV-movie moment of near-death enlightenment and reconciliation.

And I believe my father when he says she's feeling a lot better just the week before I come home for Thanksgiving and that she's only on the oxygen tank for half the day now as opposed to 24/7. I feel certain that she is on the road to recovery and I forget that she still has some cancer in the only lung she has. I fly home for Thanksgiving and arrive at an empty house and a note that says, "Went to a party at the Forestas', back around ten. Salami and provolone and some nice smoked mozz. in fridge," which I take to mean that my mother is cured, and I call my friends to discuss and analyze the miracle cure. And when my mother comes home as beautiful and put together as ever but still attached to the oxygen tank and has to sit down on the second stair from the exhaustion, I retain the assumption that she's still cured but just tired and following the precautionary miracle cure maintenance of using the oxygen and not overexerting herself. I help her up the stairs and I try to ignore how much she sounds like Grandma when she says, *I'm sorry I'm so tired. I really wanted to visit,* and I eat the cold cuts in the kitchen with my dad after she goes to sleep and when he says, *Your mother's not doing very well,* I say, *I thought she was better,* and I decide she just overdid it with the party. When he says he's going to take her to the hospital tomorrow if she's not feeling better, I put down the cold cuts.

And when Mom wakes up the next morning not feeling better and my father says he's taking her to the hospital, I remain calm as she simultaneously shrieks and rings a bell she brought with her into the bathroom in case she needs help but I silently wonder how I'm going to survive a week of simultaneous shrieking and bell-ringing. I have not forgotten how bad the shrieking sometimes was even before she got cancer and a bell. I am aware that drugs + cancer + shrieking + bell = my imminent commitment to a mental health facility. I long for the days of good old unadulterated shrieking. I am aware that $d + c + s + b =$ 10x worse than my worst nightmare, and that $x =$

a gazillion. I help her out of the tub and I do not cringe at the sight of the scar down her back that I have seen dozens of times now anyway as she hasn't lost her nudist leanings. Which sets in motion another train of thought that includes the memory of countless embarrassments beginning when I was six as a result of her nudist leanings. It includes wishing I were still six. It includes wishing my mother were still sneaking me under subway turnstiles even though I will never be mistaken for a five-year-old again and even though I hated that she did that at the time. It includes wishing Mom and I were still pretending that the Calder sculpture in Lincoln Center was an ice cream stand or a lemonade stand or a hot dog stand or any kind of a stand, or that she was still letting me stay up late *just this one time* to watch *Laugh-In* because I love Lily Tomlin even though she lets me watch it every week and I don't get half the jokes anyway because I'm six. It includes wondering what my mother was like when she was six.

I button her shirt and pull her sweater over her head and pretend not to notice that she's trying to pretend it's not as exhausting to her to hold her arms up for 2.4 seconds as it would be for me to suddenly run a marathon tomorrow. I blend in her makeup and feel reassured that I have been blending in her makeup for years now because she's had bad vision since the failed chemistry experiment when she was ten. Which is followed by wondering what my mother was like when she was ten. I finish blending in her makeup and I wish that my complexion was for even one day as good as hers is now and I ignore the irony that the person who so steadfastly avoided the sun and cigarettes came down with cancer anyway. I look for an overnight bag and when she shakes her head and says, *No, the wheelie bag is ready*, I ignore the way she has to breathe in before she says each word and also ignore that she's got a bag half-packed for times like these and I follow her instructions to pack the baby's needlepoint she hasn't finished along with the latest Robin Cook novel and some hotel stationery from a trip she took twenty years ago and her *book* and I do not remind her that she is going to the hospital and not for a week in the country. I put in a pair of pink socks, a nightie and a worn Ziploc bag with eighteen prescription bottles in it (recognizing only the ones I might personally care to ingest) and I close up the wheelie bag. I half-smile at my mother calling it a wheelie bag. Under no circumstances will I openly cry or yell or appear to have any human feeling that might make her feel worse. I tell her I love her when she gets into the car with my dad and I make a mental note that this is the first time I've ever said it first.

When my father comes home late that night and tells me my mother has pneumonia but that with antibiotics she should be home in a week, I believe him and I do not consider the reality that pneumonia + cancer + one lung = bad. I consider only that all the math problems I've been doing lately add up to bad. When he says she might miss Thanksgiving I feel grateful for curable diseases like pneumonia but remember how bummed out she was when she missed Easter and I believe the doctors one last time. Later, not so much.

When my father drops me off at the hospital the next morning to find my mother in a morphine-induced coma, I understand only that the *nurse practitioner* whatever the hell that is must be mistaken when she says, *It's just a matter of days.* I understand that she does not know me and does not know that this is *my* mother, that I have no siblings or husband or children and furthermore that things were just starting to get better with me and my mother and that I will need more time, that she will need more time, that I am sure that over the next twenty years things will naturally improve even more especially after she is miraculously cured and has life-changing revelations as a result of being cured that lead her to the serenity she hasn't quite found yet in spite of looking in a lot of places. This is followed by me explaining to the nurse practitioner that she must wake my mother up immediately so that I can talk to her and tell her that while the people at Memorial Sloan-

Kettering *seem* perfectly pleasant and all, that it is really full of quacks and liars and people with weird titles that I never heard of before and that I love her very much but she needs to snap out of it and heal now, followed by me demanding to speak to the president of the hospital and all of the scientists who thought up these horrible, painful, ineffective non-miracle cures so that I can explain that sixty-three is an unacceptable age for my mother to die, which is followed by me realizing that I have just turned into my mother.

So I call my father and when he arrives at the same time as the actual doctor who says he's so sorry, I do not cry and I do not understand for another twenty-four hours that this isn't a mistake and that she cannot be woken up. I understand only that junkies eventually wake up and I fail to see the difference. I take turns with my father holding my mother's hand for the next forty-eight hours and we do nothing besides watch her breathe because that would be wrong. When I come back from the cafeteria with my twenty-fifth cup of coffee, I notice that the old lady in the next bed is no longer there and assume she died until it occurs to me that they moved her because my mother is about to die. I meet my cousin at the door and tell her to just try to remember my mom how she was and burst into tears when she tells me her five-year-old lit a candle for her and prayed to Santa Claus and hands me a drawing with "I'm sorry" written in letters so big that the Y is on the other side.

When one of the nurses kindly suggests removing my mother's pink socks as well as the diamond ring from her fingers before she goes, I cringe, I remove both the socks and the ring and I feel like a thief. This is followed by me realizing that this is not the diamond ring I'd dreamed of owning followed by wondering about the need for removing the pink socks. When another nurse mentions that my mom could linger like this for a while and asks if I'd like the priest to come by, I look at my father and we nod vigorously at the exact same time even though I have more than a few questions about god that to date remain unanswered and as he reads the last rites I listen in confusion. When the phone rings with a call from her own minister who's on her way up and my mother takes her last meager gasp in that second, I do not fail to recognize that maybe god is in touch with my mom, even if he's crossed me off his call sheet. When the priest tells us she's with Jesus now, I manage to suppress my urge to say, *Oh really?* and follow it up with a lot of sarcastic questions. I zip up the wheelie bag and wait about a half hour before crying, followed by crying more than I ever thought possible. Followed by crying continuously for the next month, crying when things are funny and crying when people say nice things. Followed by wondering what god was thinking. Followed by wondering if god thinks.

The next day: I call everyone who needs to be called and note inappropriate responses such as dismay that my grief conflicts with someone's cocktail party. I take a call from a nice college friend I lost touch with and I appreciate her overlooking the fact that I never responded to her wedding invitation.

Day two: I wonder if it's wrong to go out to dinner followed by knowing that it is and going anyway and laughing in between crying spells followed by wondering later how I could have laughed when nothing is funny anymore.

Day three: I realize that I am marking time in "days since" now and I realize that it is Thanksgiving and I note irony again.

Day four: I realize that the outfit I brought for Thanksgiving is not also appropriate for a funeral and I think about going shopping and then I feel creeped out about shopping and then I get my cousin to go shopping for me.

Day five: I realize that the medical community is actually a medical industry.

Day six: I decide not to go to the funeral and then I go to the funeral. I sob like I did when I was a kid and didn't get my way, that way kids do when they seem like they're going to stop breathing they're sobbing so hard. I note that there are several hundred people at the funeral and I wonder if I even know several hundred people and I wonder if even several people will show up at my funeral. I feel grateful when the minister's homily reassures me that there is a god and I feel strangely reassured by her admission that she has no idea why these things happen or whether god is participating in this area at all. I appreciate that the minister speaks kindly of my mother while avoiding canonization. I consider joining this church even though I live 900 miles away and still have some dissatisfaction with god and I laugh through my tears when a dozen people of various faiths and distant cities tell me they are considering joining this church, but later I feel less certain about joining this church when my father hands me the audiotape of the homily (apparently a routine practice at this church), which to me seems like a macabre wedding video I would never want to watch.

Back at the house, I laugh with my friends like it's a party and note the overwhelming compassion of everyone present and I tell all my friends I love them. After they leave I call up everyone else I love and tell them I love them and vow to myself never to speak to anyone again who I don't completely love.

Day seven: When I find my mother's pink socks among the laundry the housekeeper has folded and put on my bed, I cry on them and put them in my suitcase.

Day nine: I go back to Chicago.

Day eleven: I go back to work.

Day twelve: When I can't stop crying, I go back to New York for two more weeks, realizing that my body is out of my control.

Month one: I join a support group and I notice that I am now marking time in "months since."

Month two: I resent anyone who still has a mom and speaks about it openly in front of me.

Month three: I notice that the people in the support group don't appreciate my sense of humor and I realize that outside of Manhattan everyone has not already been through therapy and may react by stomping out of rooms instead of laughing at my sense of humor. I burst into tears when my mom's car comes even though it's a thousand times better than my K car, which at this point doesn't even go anymore.

Month four: I cry a few times a week and quit the support group because it's depressing. I feel surprised that it's depressing. I note that aside from my three best friends, no one's calling to check up on me anymore and I assume this means I'm supposed to be over it even though I am certain that I will never be over it. I remember that when some of their mothers died, I probably didn't call them in month four. I promise myself that when the rest of their mothers die I will call to check up on them in month four.

Month five: I cry once a week, but still as hard as ever, and I decide it's okay to wear one of her sweaters now but when I notice how it still smells like her I burst into tears. This is followed by smelling her perfume bottle and then deciding that I will only smell it sparingly so that it doesn't get used up and so that it always reminds me of her.

Month six: I cry randomly, as hard as ever, and notice that I am no longer crying once a week. I realize that I am a terrible person and that this can only mean I am someday going to forget her altogether.

Month seven: I donate some of my mother's things to charity and hold a garage sale for the rest of it. I give an unfinished needlepoint, with yarn, free of charge to a nice lady who I am certain will always remember the woman she never knew who started it, but later refuse to sell a burnt potholder to a guy who haggles one too many times.

Month eight: I quit my job because life is short and I do what I want to do. I consider a backup plan, if necessary, of moving to a pleasant, remote location where there are fewer people for me to meet who could potentially die later.

Month nine: I freak out about moles and go to the dermatologist twice in a month, just to be sure.

Month ten: I have some success at what I want to do and I feel guilty and sad that my mother isn't here to see that I finally like my life except for the part about her being dead.

Month eleven: I open my mother's *book*. I find a to-do list that includes a section on the bottom head-lined XMAS underneath which it says only

D. — stuffers and pj's
H. — mono cufflinks, stuffers

at which time I remember I have a drawer full of stocking stuffers that never got stuffed and I burst into tears in a day-two fashion.

1st anniversary: I wonder why people die on holidays and whether Mom would have made it to Christmas if I'd planned to come then and I wonder if I'd never come at all if she'd still be alive, waiting for me to come and I am sure it's my fault and then I wonder if I will always mark time this way and then I become sure that I will.

Normal

MY FRIEND is fucking a girl who has a thing for knives. She likes to cut people. Sometime during the sex she likes to cut you. I am supposed to understand that these are not mortal wounds, that it's more of an erotic thing or symbolism or something and what I say to that as he smiles and says it's no big deal really is *Yet.* When I ask what he supposes happened to this girl, what happens to people who can only have sex in ways like this, ways that hurt, he says I don't know. Something. He says the girl with the thing for knives looks like a normal person and dresses like a normal person (khakis, black tee, chunky black wedgies) which in this case, in my estimation, is a disguise. (Conversely, I disguise myself with ink and vintage when the truth is I am obviously at least normal enough to be mystified by the knife thing.) The girl with the thing for knives has some kind of really normal job (anything I can't understand by title alone and characterized by the presence of benefits and little overtime and vacation pay and made-up words like *visioning*) and a normal apartment where the knives are no more conspicuous than they are at anyone else's house who has knives but not a thing for them. So I ask my friend, who is also fucking a few other girls, if anyone else noticed, and he says oh sure they have and I say what did you tell them and he says told them he walked into his car door or something. How he explained why he might have walked into his car door naked I'm not sure, because knife girl cut him on his ass and so I am thinking that when he amasses cuts on his neck and his back and his dick, and you know it's got to go that way, I am thinking this is a ruse that won't last long and I am a little concerned for him because he's a sweet guy (disguised as a player) and because he's pretty, and I'd hate to see that pretty face messed up and because he likes trouble, more than me even, and I like a little trouble.

Return
from the Depot!

NATURALLY, THERE ARE PEOPLE who think
I need counseling.

They tell me that I'm in denial. They say, *I'm here
for you.* They say, *You can call anytime just to talk.*

They suggest groups. They say, *There are support
groups for what you are going through.*

Believe me, I wish there were.

They suggest other things. Yoga. Transcendental medi-
tation. Reiki. Sacrocranial massage. Medication. They
say, *You should go to a spa. Take a vacation. Take a
class.* They look at me with their heads tilted. They
give me earnest looks. They say, *Three years is a long*

time, it might be time to let go. I'm not angry with them. Some of them have lost people too. But there's something they don't understand. My mother is coming back.

I realize that this doesn't happen often.

They give me books. I have read the Kübler-Ross book. Okay, well, to be honest I read it in college. This time I just kind of skimmed it — denial, anger, bargaining, depression, acceptance. As I said, the collective belief is that I'm stuck in the denial phase when in fact, my belief is that this is just a big mistake that will eventually be straightened out. If anything I'm in phase two because I have quite a bit of a bone to pick with whoever's in charge and frankly I'd be willing to strike all kinds of bargains if I knew who that was. But it's hard to be depressed when you know with absolute certainty that sooner or later the person who everyone else thinks is dead is coming back. There's nothing to be depressed about. And there's certainly nothing to accept.

I consulted the Ouija board. I never got anything much except consonants. Once I got MNOT which I interpreted every which way but never made any definite conclusions. Monotony? Mom not? Mom not what? Susan Minot? I read that book of hers about her mom dying but couldn't find any clues there either, and of course that book depicts the traditional, mom-dies-people-get-upset kind of scenario. I thought about going to Minot, North Dakota, but it seemed like a long way to go without some kind of guarantee.

I went to psychics. I thought a psychic would be the first to see my point of view, to say, *Of course it was a terrible mistake,* and that they would then immediately locate the perpetrators of the mistake, that they would say something like, *You need to go speak with Fritz Miller in the accounting department at Kidder Peabody. He'll give you the appropriate paperwork and straighten the whole thing out.* But they don't; they, too, offer earnest sentiments and tilted heads and the best they'll do is say, *She wants you to know she's fine. She's in a better place.* And when I'd ask for the exact location of the better place they say things like *the other side,* which isn't of much use, and I spent a lot of time trying to figure out the other side of *what?*

So I stopped talking about it so much. I try to put on sad looks to make them think I'm okay. Which of course, is a fairly ridiculous concept, when you think about it. I did go to a group, briefly, right after Mom "died," but it was depressing. They were all *sobbing,* talking about their *feelings,* talking about *moving on.* Some of them had lost sisters and children. And I mean, I can't say for sure whether those people actually died or not, I do understand that people die, most of my grandparents have died, and I didn't want to offend anyone, but I really wanted to say, *Have you thought about looking for them? Are you so sure they're gone for good?* In my case, my mom is too young, that's part of why I'm sure this mistake was made, but it certainly is more understandable when the parents go first, that is the natural order of things. But when younger people and especially when children die, I wouldn't be so quick to call that the end of it. That just doesn't make sense. But I kept my opinion to myself, because by the time I went to the support group it was about a year afterward and my friends and family had already made it clear that they thought maybe I shouldn't mention the thing about my mom not really being dead, you know, that that might not go over so well in a grief support group.

I've been back at work since shortly after the funeral, more earnest looks and whispers, and I try to keep her house up as best I can, which is sometimes hard because I live in Chicago and the house is in New Jersey, but I go back a few times a year and I have a gardener and a housekeeper come every once in a while so the place will look nice when she gets back. I did eventually cancel her subscriptions and her cable, which seemed silly to pay for not knowing exactly when she'd be back, and I took the dog, because obviously a dog can't stay alone for more than a day. And, well, I borrowed a few other things, like the TV from the den, when mine blew out, and a set of brand-new sheets I didn't think she'd miss, and her jewelry. (Which was a mistake because I was later burglarized, and although I did get some of it back, the box with the rings in it was never returned. So the only ring I have now is the one I was wearing that day, my grandmother's "mother" ring, with a diamond in the center and two pink stones on either side representing her two daughters.)

My mother's friends and family grieved. They sobbed, they went to groups, they *accepted.* I waited. And as it turned out, I was right. Mom came back.

Things were a little different than I expected.

She'd been waiting in a bus depot sixty miles southeast of Minot, North Dakota. How about that? She was told that there were delays. That there were weather problems. That there were engine problems. That there were traffic problems. I said, *For three years?* She said, *Tell me about it.* Then she said, *Finally they admitted there was a mix-up with my ticket. Your ticket?* I said. *Yes,* she said, *I only got a one-way.* I asked how she got there. She said, *There's a tunnel system.* I said, *What do you mean, tunnel system?* She said, *There's a tunnel system underground that shuttles people out of graveyards when mistakes like these are made that go to this bus depot*

*in North Dakota, and from there you're supposed to
get a ticket back to wherever you came from. But in
this case another mistake was made.*

I knew it! I said.

*Fuckers fed me coffee out of vending machines
and those nasty cheese crackers for three years.*

Mom, you used to love those cheese crackers.

*You try living on cheese crackers and coffee with
"whitener" for three years. It's not nutritious.*

Mom, I said, *I'm just so glad to see you.*

I'm glad to see you too, sweetheart, she said. *Is
there any mail?*

I tried to explain that everyone on the planet besides me had thought she was dead all this time, thus
the lack of mail.

Well, Christ, she said, *that's quite an assumption
to make.*

I know! I said.

Where's doggie?

He's in the yard. Mom ran to the yard and yelled
for the dog, who came running. *Doggie! My doggie!
Mama's baby doggie! I missed you so much! Mama's
doggie do. Poor baby, missed his mama! Yes I'm here!
Mama's here!*

Now, it was about in the middle of the dog reunion
that I realized I didn't get so much as a hug a few
minutes before when Mom came back. Which was
weird, because she used to be pretty huggy with me. I

will admit, she always had a weird relationship with the dog. But you know, she'd been *dead.* It's not like she just went out of town. Weirdest of all, I felt a little jealous. I'd been starting to feel like the dog was mine.

Anyway, the neighbors saw us in the yard and of course they were beside themselves, because unlike me, no one was expecting this. The Marksons next door, whose son I used to babysit, walked over crying hysterically, and seemed confused. Mom tried to explain just as Ginny the religious fanatic from up the street walked by with her dog, screaming at the sight of my mother. She crossed herself and actually fell down on the grass screaming some prayers or something. Later that day we figured it was Ginny who called the local news stations, because suddenly there were half a dozen trucks with those big extending antennas or whatever they are, breaking the branches off the trees, which you can be sure that my mother yelled at them about. Those trees are about a hundred years old. Anyway, my mother *invited them in,* the reporters, put on a big pot of coffee, and held a press conference in the living room. She explained the whole story about the bus depot and the cheese crackers and not one of them asked any kind of pressing question about how unbelievable the story was, suddenly everyone seemed to have no questions about what they wanted to institutionalize me for saying not too long before. They were like, *Bus depot, underground shuttle, sure.* And she had the death certificate, and she told them if there was any question at all to call the doctors, and the minister who gave her eulogy, and everyone who came to her funeral and saw her in the coffin three years ago looking pretty dead. And they did check that all out and it was all verified although there was curiously no evidence of the bus depot in question or for that matter any other returned-from-the-dead people. But no one questioned that my mother was back. She obviously was.

Out of all the hoopla came an unexpected bonus as far as my mother was concerned. She became a celebrity. She went on talk shows. She gave interviews. It seemed to extend past the allotted fifteen minutes. And then it happened. My mother got an offer to have her own TV show, a sitcom based on her life/death/return from the bus depot. That's what they called it, actually. *Return from the Depot!* Featuring my mom as herself, and a little Bichon Frise as "Doggie," and Lindsay Wagner as Ginny the religious fanatic and Alyssa Milano playing me. *I know.*

My mother was never an actress. She was, briefly, on the pageant circuit in Iowa, where she grew up. She had played classical piano in high school, won a few pre–Miss Iowa pageants, and then met my dad when she went to college when she was about eighteen and had me a few years after that. When they got divorced she moved to New York intending to be a concert pianist, and she was talented and got some work, but never got the recognition she craved. So she taught from the time I was about ten. Anyway, she obviously saw the show as her chance, and she got them to write it into the script, the piano thing, but I think she was more excited about being famous than anything else.

Of course the show was a big hit. There was a lot of curiosity, even though it really wasn't all that much different from any other sitcom, although I will say that my mother always had the potential to be a star. She probably should have gone into acting long ago, because she always had a diva thing going on. So she was a natural.

At the end of the show's first season they brought in Alan Thicke for a guest spot and he fell madly in love with Mom right away, sent her all kinds of crazy flowers and gifts, and it took her all of about three months to agree to marry him. I couldn't blame her for wanting to be with someone. But I was a little jealous. All that time I'd been waiting for her to come back, I thought we'd get to spend more time together. I had a long time to think about how stupid I'd been so many times, what a waste of time it was, blaming her for everything that was wrong in my life. It didn't occur to me that she was just a person who wanted a kid but maybe didn't realize what that would really involve. I thought if she came back I'd be a better daughter. I thought she'd be a better mother. I thought, dying and coming back, especially after being gone so long, it would have to change things. You would just naturally want to make things right. I think there were other things she was trying to make right. I wasn't included.

So I eventually went back to Chicago, which was quite a bit lonelier than ever without the dog. Alan moved in with Mom and she'd call once every week or so to say hi and tell me what the dog was doing and then she'd get off the phone giggling because Alan was trying to have sex with her all the time including whenever she got on the phone with me.

And then the other day I went to the supermarket and when I got inside the store I took off my glove and happened to notice that one of the pink stones was missing from my grandmother's ring. And I'm not one who ever sees a lot of signs (in spite of this whole mom-coming-back thing I don't have an overall mystical kind of life outlook) but I called Mom immediately from my cell phone and Alan answered and I asked if Mom was there and he said, *Who?* and I said, *Mom, your wife, Mrs. Thicke,* and he said, *I don't know who you are or how you got this number young lady but most people know I'm married to Carmen Electra and I'm going to contact my security company immediately.* So I called her at work but the woman who answered sounded an awful lot like Mrs. C.

from *Happy Days,* and she was pleasant with me but she hung up as soon as she said, *I think you have the wrong number.* I called the Marksons, who said, *Sweetie, we thought you let this go already.* I called Ginny the religious fanatic who said something about *messing with god's will* and said a Hail Mary and hung up on me. I ran to the checkout counter to look at the *TV Guide.* I looked up the listing for *Return from the Depot!* And there was a big ad for the show with a picture of Mrs. Cunningham with the rest of the cast, no mention of my mother, and no indication that she was just replaced or something. It seems clear she was never there.

Now, I know what you're thinking. You're thinking this is the part where I realize, via a simple metaphor, that my mother is not coming back, the part where I snap out of my denial and realize that there will be no big reunion, that she will not send me vitamins or make me chicken soup again when I'm sick, or buy me a new teakettle when mine gets rusty, where I realize that we will never go outlet shopping again, never decorate another Christmas tree, that we will never again giggle uncontrollably about my cousin's famously cheap Christmas presents like the orange garage sale bodysuit she sent my mom one year with the $3 tag still on it that I made her try on that made her look like a demented superhero, where I understand that I will never get to show her the home movies from my childhood that Dad put on video that I forgot to bring to Jersey the last time before she died, understand that the plane ticket she bought to Chicago will never get used, that when the plane ticket is not used we will not be having coffee on my porch, that she'll never get to meet Bob or Lisa or Michael and that they'll never get to meet her, that we will never trash another distant relative's poor fashion choices, where I understand that I will never get to tell her that I met the guy from *The Young and the Restless* she always liked, never get to tell her about some great boyfriend (hypothetical), that I will never get to tell her that even though she was completely crazy that I would never in a million years want any other mom, that Mrs. C. would pale in comparison, the part where I realize that I will never get to ask her all the questions I wanted to ask her, like where is the touch-up paint to the station wagon, like how do you knit a popcorn stitch, like the exact basil-to-oregano ratio for the perfect marinara, like how come I have no brothers or sisters, like what was I like when I was a kid, was I a bad kid? I'm sorry if I was a bad kid, like what were you like when you were a kid, you were probably a good kid, the best kid, like what was life like during wartime, what was it like to have two parents, what was Grandma like then, like what was it that made you so sad sometimes, the part where I understand I can't discuss her funeral with her like it was a party, tell her how many people came and what they were wearing and what asshole didn't show up because he had a birthday party to go to, where I understand that I can't ask her what was it like for her when Grandma died, the part where I understand why my mother wasn't there to help me get through my mother's death, because it still makes perfect sense to me that anyone would need their mom at a time like that. But it isn't. It's the part where I go to the jeweler's.

I didn't bother explaining the whole story to the jeweler but I gave them an extra hundred bucks to put in a new stone while I waited. I told them it had to be exactly like the other one or I'd take my business elsewhere. They replaced the stone. It looked good.

I waited again.

I got a phone call from my aunt. She said, *Hi, this is Aunt Marni.* She seemed cheerful. She seemed to have moved on.

I said, *Hi Aunt Marni.*

She said, *Hold on, there's someone who wants to talk to you.*

I held on.

Then again she said, *Hi, this is Aunt Marni.*

I said, *Aunt Marni, I thought you were going to put someone on the phone.*

She said, *I did, I put myself on the phone.*

Aunt Marni was trying to make a point.

I was missing it. I said so. She explained.

I duplicated Aunt Marni.

She asked if I knew anything about it.

I told her I thought I might but I sure as hell didn't know how to fix it.

She said, *Fix it? This is the best thing that ever happened to me! No more sex with Uncle Edgar! Ha!*

I hung up the phone.

I flew to North Dakota. I rented a car and drove to every bus station south of Minot and showed people pictures of my mom and no one claimed to have seen her although one said she looked a lot like a Junior Miss Muscatine County she once knew. I was pretty close to giving it up just out of exhaustion. Finally I found a guy who said there had been someone there who looked like her, and I ended up explaining the entire situation, from the depot to the aunt duplication, and it seemed like maybe I was going to get the earnest head-tilt again, but instead I got a long pause and a lip-purse. I thought he wasn't going to say anything at all, the pause was so long, but he finally said, *That's a sad story. I'm sorry that happened to you. And* it was hard to tell whether he really believed me or not but he could obviously tell that I needed someone to believe me, and I'm grateful to him for that. It gave me just the motivation I needed to keep going. I drove all the way to New Jersey to look around the neighborhood for her one more time. No luck.

Aunt Marni and Aunt Marni are still living it up. Mom hasn't come back again. Yet.

But at least I got the dog back.

The Daves

LATELY, I have been dating guys named Dave.

Probably, I should just write: The End right here. It hasn't escaped me that the Dave name has certain implications, multiples thereof notwithstanding. That if I were to write instead, "Lately, I have been dating *a* guy named Dave," you'd probably still picture some sort of slacking/short-sleeve-shirt-wearing/senior-year-backpacking-in-Europe scenario. Whereas if I had said, "Lately I have been dating a guy named David," you would maybe say, "Hm, I wonder what this story is going to be about," you might even edit in your head, you might go, "Perhaps the word *man* in place of the word *guy* would have been a better

115

choice." Before you even read the rest of the David story, you would just know that any complications that ensued would be sophisticated and adult in nature, as a result of David the corporate lawyer who lavishes expensive gifts on me being maybe inherently uptight and having, like, dry-cleaned socks or underwear or something.

As opposed to:

The Daves:

Dave #1: Twenty-four years old. Freelance graphic artist. Smoker. One tattoo. Three roommates, one female. Occasional laundry-oriented absence of underwear.

Dave #2: Thirty. Something to do with the Internet. (Believe me, if I had any ideas beyond that I'd say so.) Smoker. Wears sandals. Frequent choice-oriented absence of underwear.

Dave #3: Thirty-one. Finishing graduate degree in religion. Smoker. Refers to futon as "bed." Cat. Presence of underwear unknown.

Me:

Almost forty-one. Preschool teacher. Nonsmoker. Ink-free. Large drawer devoted entirely to underwear.

A Brief History of the Occurrence and Relationship Trajectory of Each Dave

Ways in Which Dave #1 Succeeded on Date #1:

1. Appeared fascinated by everything I said.
2. Seemed unconcerned about significant age difference.
3. Paid for dinner.
4. Creative post-dinner suggestion of roller-skating.

Ways in Which Dave #1 Subsequently
  Became an Obvious Mismatch:

1. Lack of car/residency at a remote distance.
2. Three roommates, one female.
3. Unwillingness to relinquish belief that Valentine's Day is the product of a vast conspiracy between Hallmark and the federal government.
4. Re: "Ways in Which Dave #1 Succeeded on Date #1," point #2 and the word *seemed*, Dave #1 eventually mentioned the age difference as potentially being a problem

which

  a) I knew

and

  b) I hadn't mentioned since it seemed obvious and unnecessary but

        c) he likes to *talk about it,* which arguably is both very

          i) yin on his part and somewhat appreciated

but also

          ii) sometimes talk is overrated.

And then there's also his

        5. Tendency toward impulsive behavior such as

          a) striking up conversations with strangers

which is endearing until he

          b) casually mentions some detail from our sex life

although sometimes

          c) he brings ice cream and raspberries after a fight, which is kind of sweet.

Reasons Why Dave #2 Is Still
in the Picture but Some Others
Indicating Maybe He Shouldn't Be:

1. Always pays, in spite of the fact that we haven't kissed yet and it's been a while.
2. Writes long, funny e-mails.
3. Says I'm "empirically beautiful" and that I smell good.
4. Has job.

5. Tendency toward unlicensed, uncontracted psychotherapy.
6. Watched *Tomb Raider* on first date (downloaded from Internet).

Ways in Which Dave #3 Failed on Date #1:

1. Showed me his bed.
2. At the movies,
   a) after a failed attempt to position himself on line so that I'd reach the ticket window first
   b) paid only for his own ticket

and although I'm sure it was not his intention to make me feel both uncared-for and elderly, when he paid with

   c) his student discount

that was the result.

3. Took me to 7-Eleven after the movie for a Slurpee

which

   a) was fine with me, I like Slurpees

but

   b) he didn't pay for that either

and

   c) a Slurpee costs like, 99 cents

and

   i) I have enforced, after much experi-

mentation and consideration, a "whoever asks, pays" rule

and frankly

ii) though my quasi-feminist leanings
cause me a little trouble on this
front, it's just nice when they pay

4. Took me on "romantic" walk in rodent-
infested park

at which point it was pretty much over.

I decide to date someone without the Dave name.

This turns out to be something of a problem.

I go to a bar with my girlfriend.

Nothing but Daves.

I'm not speaking metaphorically.

After the fourth or fifth Dave I start to suspect some
joke, but my girlfriend denies it, so I ask just about
every guy in the bar what his name is. "Dave." "Dave."
"Dave." "Dave." "Dave." "Dave." "Dave." "Dave."
"Dave."

We go to another bar. More Daves.

We go to a gay bar. Daves there.

I ask her what she thinks about this. She says, Well, they kind of are all the same.

No, I'm not one of those women. I'm not one of those women who thinks all guys are the same. I am *open-minded.*

No you're not, says my friend.

I didn't say that out loud, I say.

She shrugs.

I look at a newspaper. The headline: "Dave Clinton Moves into Harlem Office."

People magazine: "Dave Clooney Is the Sexiest Man Alive," again.

At the bookstore: titles by Dave Updike, Dave Mailer, Dave Rushdie.

Don't you find this weird? I ask my friend.

She says, It doesn't really bother me. She says, Maybe you should just relax. There are some nice Daves out there.

I didn't say there weren't.

All right, look, she says. I do know this one guy named Steve . . .

Steve? Is that better than Dave?

He doesn't smoke. No cats. Centrally located.

Aw, that's just a well-disguised Dave.

I hear he's especially skilled in certain areas.
Where do you hear these things? Really?
My friend Jennifer used to date him.
Steve it is.

Ways in Which Steve Didn't Seem That Much Different from a Dave at First:

1. First date free concert in the park which would have been fine

except that

2. It rained

and

3. It was Dave Matthews

and Dave Matthews is okay but of course this gets into the whole Dave weirdness again and I guess

4. People who really like Dave Matthews also like the Dave Matthews rain experience

and of course, more often than not

5. Wear sandals.

And then

Some Weird Things Happened While Dave Matthews Was Singing "Crazy"

1. Steve called me Jennifer.

To which I said

2. My name isn't Jennifer.

And Steve laughed like I was joking and so again I said, My name isn't Jennifer, and he said

3. Everyone's name is Jennifer, what are you
   talking about?

And I said one more time, My name isn't Jennifer.
And some girl next to me said something like, Well
goody for you, at which point I asked her name and of
course she said, *Jennifer,* in italics like that, like *what
else?*

And it was then that

The Clouds Parted
(literally/figuratively)

And I said, Steve, what are you doing tomorrow
night? Do you want to go to a movie? My treat? And
he said, You just called me Steve. To which I said, I
know, and he said, But my name is Dave.

And I said, So what do you say?

The End

He Thinks He Thinks

I KNOW WHAT HE'S THINKING. And he knows that I know what he's thinking most of the time because after all these years we have a way of communicating silently with our eyes and right now I know he's thinking I'm still thinking about him and that I'll never stop thinking about him and maybe that's true and maybe it isn't. Maybe I will always be thinking that he's really in love with me. That there's an *in* in the sentence. I don't know. He thinks if he says I love you and means it as a friend which I know he does, he thinks if he says this that there will be interpretation, that I will hear the *in* in the sentence whether it's there or not but I'm not stupid. I may go ahead and think that he is really in love with me but I will never again think that he's going to be with me. I know that we will go on with our lives and become involved with many or several or with any luck just two other people (one per), people with whom we will be awake at the same time and when we meet parents he will not refer to me as his *friend* and we will be happy and he will tell me he loves me and there will always be an *in* in the sentence and maybe there will even be beautiful babies but I will know that we had that thing even though he thinks he thinks that we didn't have that thing, even though he thinks he thinks that it was never a full-on thing, that it was another thing, a thing that had something to do with us being in the right place at the right time for this particular greater purpose, that god may have been involved even, but not for the other thing, not for love. (And I know why he thinks that and I get it, I do, it's just that I don't think the possible god thing is exclusive of the other thing, the love.) But I know what he really thinks because I see the way he looks at me, even when I'm looking at someone else I know he's looking at me, and I know he doesn't have a jealous bone in his body which can be annoying at times, but still, I know that he looks at me looking at these other people and he just keeps looking at me that way, and he thinks he thinks that this is just him being happy for me, happy that I'm moving on and looking at other people, but on some other level, a level he won't admit to, not even to himself, I think he thinks that it should be him, and I think it should be him and I think it should be me, but what we both know is that it won't. It won't be him and it won't be me. We have many things in common and many things not in common and I know that the not-in-common things are more heavily considered on his part than they are on mine. I think we can *work things out*. He thinks we cannot. I think the things we have in common are more sort of profound worldview things and the things we don't have in common are lifestyle things, although now that I think about it there may be some overlap, there may be some little bits of his profound worldview where I drift off (tendency toward spontaneous public nakedness as expression of comfort in world [and/or humor]/smoking is cool) but nevertheless when I see him with these other people, these wrong people, I think that he should be with me. And I think he knows this on a level he won't admit to I can see it when he looks at me.

Christina

MY APARTMENT IS HAUNTED by the ghost
of a baby named Christina. I had been living here for
a couple of years already when I first saw her, right
around the time Joe and I decided to take a break. I
think after a year of hearing him plead, *Christina,
Christina*, she couldn't take it anymore and finally
said, *What?* as he was on his way out the door.
Christina is my name, too.

So there's this ghost baby standing there looking
up at me and the first thing she said was, *I'm sorry
you're having a bad day, man*. Naturally I was a little
nonplussed, to say the least, and thought I was surely
hallucinating until she showed me some of her special
powers, which include scaring the squirrels out of my

flowers and giving me blond highlights that don't dry out my hair. (I would later hear, at length, about exactly what ghosts could and couldn't do; it was Christina's idea to someday write a treatise on this topic demystifying the stereotypical ghost images in popular culture, which really bugged her. Among things ghosts don't do, I would discover, are walking through walls, carrying chains, and moaning all the time [*what's the point of that nonsense?* she said, *there's no* pain *here*]; she swore to me that no one she knows would ever have cause to say "Boo." Christina's biggest gripe, though, was the whole thing about "seeing the light" when you die, the idea that there was some big moment of spiritual enlightenment *with angels or some shit*, she said. *That's all crap.*) Also I'd like to clarify, in my limited experience with ghosts, that she isn't transparent at all, she's completely opaque, although she does have the ability to make herself invisible on an as-needed basis, which you may have already guessed tends to coincide with my attempts to introduce her to people. *I'm not really a people person*, she said.

I hear that, I said.

The last time I went out some lady tried to drag me to her church with some loony idea that she was going to stick me in a manger for the benefit of worshippers wanting to get my blessing, like they do every time statues of Mary start crying or when the face of Jesus appears on a potato. I'm not Jesus, I told her.

I can see that, I said.

Christina told me the story of how she died (and in spite of what she said, I think she was glad for the conversation), from a fall off the porch about a week after she'd learned to walk. Her mother hadn't gotten into the habit of latching the screen door and out Christina went, exploring, onto the porch and tumbling down the stairs, landing in one of the neighbor's potted plants. *You know that lady,* she said, *the one who takes the pictures of the babies in clay pots, with flowers on their heads and stuff?*

Sure, I said.

Well, it was like that, only bad. My mom moved out right away, she said. *She didn't know I was still here.*

Let me make one thing really clear right now. Admittedly, I spend a good deal of time examining the ways in which my emotional and intellectual disposition is unique. But I'm not crazy. This isn't something that's going on in my imagination because I want to have a baby or because someone e-mailed me one of those digital dancing babies (that bear no resemblance whatsoever to Christina, who, aside from the ghost thing, is quite lifelike). Frankly, I don't know whether or not I want to have a baby *or* get married, as I am certain that I have been culturally brainwashed into thinking that I want to get married and have a baby, and that any free thought I might have about it is colored by all that other stuff, and plus, not having gotten married at this point, when it's getting closer to the time when I will have to rely on technology (and how I feel about all that is another complication entirely) or some other means of producing a baby (theft?), and you know, sometimes these days I'm exhausted just watering the plants. Anyway, she doesn't tell me to spread the word of the Lord, or that there are governmental conspiracies against me (okay, but well, although . . . never mind); Christina is a real, whole separate person who happens to be dead. The thing about her is that she has this extremely serious look on her face 90 percent of the time. She laughs and smiles like any baby, *but not unless she has a good reason.* You can easily see her looking around and observing the weirdnesses of the world that a lot of people don't seem to notice. She doesn't look miserable. She just doesn't smile all the time. People have been saying to me, *Smile, Chrissie, smile,* since forever, and it's a huge pet peeve of mine, and I say, *Just because I'm not smiling doesn't mean I'm not happy.* It means I'm not smiling. God. But you know, no one ever believes me. Anyway so what I'm saying is she has this really serious look on her face, the same way

I do in countless childhood photographs (and home movies, in which any number of great things happen, like riding a tricycle for the first time, which I am clearly enjoying [as indicated by furious pedaling and clapping] in spite of the absence of a traditional facial expression of happiness), and I could see by looking at her that she knows like I do that some things are really wrong. (I know that she can see that some things are perfectly right as well, but I really was having a bad day.) Plus she wears this peach-colored knit dress with a matching cardigan that's cute enough but for some reason it makes her look like an old lady. (Why it is her superpowers don't include a wardrobe change, I can't say.) As it is, she doesn't have that baby waddle. She walks like an old lady, kind of pitched forward, and when she falls down, usually on her face, she doesn't cry, and if you try to help her up, she says, *I'm fine, don't worry about it,* and gets up by herself.

Do you want to tell me what's going on with you? she asked. I told her I was having problems with my boyfriend. She nodded, the weighty nod of a blues singer. I told her that Joe and I had been having some problems for a little while.

He's a decent guy, I told her, *but you know, he just stays up so late.* Christina nodded again. *And all we ever do is rent movies. And then he says how bad they are, and in what way, and then how bad all the art is, on and on until we've covered the mediocrity of the entire universe, and I'm completely exhausted. We could go to bed so much earlier if he'd just say, "Yes, that was a bad movie, all the people are bad, everywhere, good night," but it's never like that.* To be fair, for the most part Joe doesn't take his dismay with the universe out on me, still, it just wears me down. Plus he says "I says" all the time. At first I thought it was kind of working-class sexy. Then no. So we'd sort of decided to take a break. It's possible that he may not have been clear on why. It's possible that *I* may not have been clear on why. It may just have been something to do. I'd been at somewhat of a general loss as to what to do about anything at that point. It may or may not be coincidental that our breakup took place on the first anniversary of my mom's death, and even though I had sort of antici-pated that that might be a sadder day than every other day, I was also at the same time thinking that because of my unique emotional and intellectual dis-position, I would be thus exempt from having these disproportionately large death-anniversary feelings, which it turns out I wasn't.

I bet you miss your mom too, she said.

You knew about that? I asked.

I am a ghost, Christina reminded me.

So, what, you're omniscient?

No, she said, *but you know, word gets around.*

Word? What are you saying?

We have some mutual acquaintances.

Well Christ, can you take me to wherever she is?

Mmm, no. You can't go that way. Anyway, apparently she moved on a while ago.

Moved on to where? I pulled the curtains closed when it occurred to me the neighbors might see me talking to what appeared to them to be no one.

That part I'm a little sketchy on. There's talk, but no one really tells you until you get there. Word has it it isn't bad. Anyway, give yourself a break. It was only a year ago, she said. My mind wrapped around the word *only* for a little while and I couldn't think of what else to say. *Let's go dance,* Christina said. I thought it seemed kind of inappropriate at that moment but she stood firm. *I want to dance.*

Even with the old-lady walk, Christina moves pretty fast, so I put on some James Brown. Her dancing is similar to her smiling. She wiggles her butt a little, and then every fourth or fifth wiggle she throws up her hands and waves them around for a second, but there isn't very much more smiling involved in the dance than there is at any other time. I followed her lead, which got a little laugh. I may not have been as good at it as she was.

She hung around for a while. I continued to go about my business but found myself making a lot of excuses (more than usual, even) to people in favor of staying home with Christina. I liked her. We rented videos and went to bed early.

Christina, I said one night, *do you ever just feel totally different?* For a second I thought she wasn't going to say anything, because the look on her face was enough to remind me who I was talking to.

Then she said, *Are you joking?*

Fair enough, I said.

The thing is, Chris, everyone feels like that.

Everyone might feel like that, I said, *but I really am.*

You're not, she said. *But your feelings are understandable.*

Is that so.

Yes. For starters, you're an only child.

Christina, I said, *I've been through therapy already.*

I'm just saying you have no verification. Siblings, within the family structure, provide a sort of reference. A kind of proof.

You're scaring me a little bit.

I may go into the psychology field, later.

A fine choice, I said.

Further, having lost a parent contributes to the feelings of isolation already in place.

I don't want to talk about that, I said.

You're not a pioneer in this area.

What?

134

People die. People get sad. You're not the inventor of that.

I'm the only daughter of a somewhat strange and unusual person who died, and no one could possibly know what that's like.

Um. Your dad? Anyone else who knew her?

Not the same. I'm not saying it's better, I said.

You think no one else feels that way and it isn't true.

Shut up.

At that point in the increasingly Pinteresque conversation, Christina burst into tears. I kept forgetting she was a baby, and I said shut up to her and she burst into tears, wailing, actually, as babies do. I didn't know what to do really, because it seemed so uncharacteristic in spite of her being a baby, but she eventually climbed up onto my lap and got her arms around me as best she could, sobbing into my sleeve. I rubbed her head and rocked her for a while, and said I was sorry about a hundred times. She finally accepted my apology but again she said, *You're not different. You're the same.*

I don't want to be the same.

Ah.

At Christmas I got us a tree and dug out my collection of ornaments. Mom and Grandma had made most of them over the years, giving me a new bunch every year in my stocking. The last few years when Mom was sick she didn't have so much energy anymore and started ordering them from mail-order catalogs. I hadn't put up a tree last year because it was so soon after she died and the Christmas spirit eluded me. Naturally, with Christina here this year, I couldn't not put up a tree. Anyway, though, I found this batch of ornaments my mom had ordered, little Christmas cookies; snowmen, candy canes, and such, that were coated with polyurethane so they could be kept and reused. Except when I took them out of the box (suspiciously light), they were all crumbly and full of tiny holes, eaten right through the polyurethane by some kind of mealy bugs, those bugs you never actually see but that leave these extensive little empty trails. Christina could see I was upset, and so she made up a rhyme to cheer me up. (*Mealy bugs mealy bugs, you're just a bunch of thugs, you can take away my stuff, but you're just dumb and pasty, because there are plenty of ornaments that aren't so tasty.*) She was a smart baby and her rhymes were good but she was still working on her meter, obviously, and felt better when I told her not all poems rhyme anyway.

We had lengthy discussions about the meaning of life. I had a notion to write some of her thoughts down, because they were very bestsellery. She had a knack for making up slogans — the one she said to me most often was "Let go or fall down," which at first I didn't get, especially coming from a baby who often fell down when she wasn't holding on to something, a baby who, you know, died from falling down. I kept trying to convince her to change it to "Let go *and* fall down," and she kept telling me I was missing the point, which kind of did take a long time to register. Other slogans included "If you don't like what you see you're probably looking in a mirror." When I pointed out that her favorite, "Life isn't so long, you know," sort of contradicted my favorite "What's the rush?" she said, *Think so?* I guessed she didn't, really. Anyway, it seemed to me like no more suspension of disbelief would be required to receive the wisdom of a dead talking baby than some guy who expects you to believe he sat down and chatted with god. But her ideas were sort of general — she didn't have any better of an idea about what love was than I did. The only point of reference she had was her father (who lasted for a week or two after Christina's conception) and a couple she met after she became a ghost who were killed (in a roller-blading mishap) who seemed truly in love, although she questioned their habit of dressing identically. A lot of the other dead people, she said, were all too happy to be rid of some of their former partners. I asked her if there was any dating in the afterlife and she said there was but it didn't seem to be a noticeable improvement.

Joe left a bunch of messages, even though we were

on this break. He seemed like he genuinely missed me and wanted to try to work things out. Christina had never met him, but she tried a bunch of times to get me to invite him over; I just couldn't. I hadn't told him about her, and I know he loves kids (although I'm not sure how he feels about ghosts); that wasn't it so much as I just wanted her to myself, even the idea of her. I'm sure the thought briefly crossed my mind that he wouldn't see her at all and wouldn't believe that I did, but honestly I was more afraid that he *would,* and that if he got to know her he might have something I wasn't sure I wanted him to have, and I couldn't explain that to either of them.

Well, at least call him back, Christina finally said.

I left him a message when I knew he wouldn't be home; it was kind of awkward and dopey. I couldn't think of anything to say. *I'm just calling you back,* I think I said. Naturally he called right back and left another bunch of messages I didn't return, and then he stopped calling altogether for a couple of weeks, which was more of a bummer than I expected, still, I wasn't especially motivated to call him again. Christina and I were having a really good time. Finally he showed up at my door one day with some flowers, not his general thing (he was more of a meaningful book kind of guy), and it was really sweet and I was tempted to talk, but I just couldn't let him in, not having told him about Christina. I said, *I think I need a little more time for me right now,* which sounded horribly hollow and TV-movieish as soon as I said it, and between that and Christina, I felt like he'd think I'd been lying to him. Okay, which I was, but that wasn't our original problem, which was him getting upset with me all the time. I might not have mentioned that he wasn't abusive or he didn't call me names or anything, it wasn't like that at all, more like he'd get extremely frustrated because, he said, I kept things to myself. I've always fancied myself a big talker, and I could never figure out what he could have wanted that I wasn't giving him. I told him everything. *It's not about what you say,* he'd say.

When I mentioned this to Christina she said, *He wants to know how you feel,* and I was like, *But I tell him that all the time,* and she just shook her head. Like she was my mother, but not the mother I had when I had a mother, who would never have butted into my love life. Even if I had mentioned it to her. (Particularly impossible, though, when said mother isn't informed that there even is a boyfriend.) *He doesn't know,* she said.

Okay, now, I understood that, but when a baby is essentially siding with your boyfriend, the *ghost* of a baby, I have to say, it's a little upsetting. But I hadn't lost anyone close to me before my mom died and quite frankly, I couldn't possibly have imagined how much it would suck and also I would have had no way of knowing that I would instantaneously realize that anyone I knew could die anytime, I would not ever have guessed that I would become obsessed with combing obituaries of any people under retirement age for the word *cancer* (about nine out of every ten), I would not have thought that I would write letters to a dozen astrologists at publications around the country asking them to remove the cancer sign from their forecasts or at least change the name (citing bad karma as my primary argument, which I figured might be a reasonable way to appeal to the astrologists), I might not have noticed that there seemed to be one continuous broadcast about that Tour de France guy who triumphed over his cancer of everything (implying it was some sort of matter of will or something, which I kept thinking, *Oh really because I'm sure if they'd informed us about that cure at Sloan-Kettering we would have checked it out*) but a suspicious lack of information about whether or not my bitterness over the entire month dedicated to breast cancer awareness (the pink Princess phone of cancers) was in any way normal at all. I wasn't so much interested in remodeling our entire calendar to include a cancer-of-the-month so much as I just got into a kind of shouting thing during the interminable month of October, when I began screaming at the TV to just fucking cure all the fucking cancers. I enjoy having breasts, but I'm just going to go ahead and say that my mother, like many people, enjoyed having *lungs*. (And it was not possible to convince me that because of the association with smoking that the cancer-curing/awareness/ fundraising people thought the lung-cancer-afflicted people [the rotary phone of cancers?] got what they deserved when, in fact, vast numbers of people like my mother held such an enjoyment of breathing that they never took up smoking and came down with lung cancer anyway.) I would not have guessed that after someone dies I wouldn't just cry for a month or two and then say, *Well there's nothing I can do*, but instead cry for a month or twelve or more and then also talk to her photos (which, unlike Christina, do not talk back), and repeatedly ask her to just come back, making all kinds of deals with the photos, completely believing that somehow via my negotiating with the photos she would actually come back (having no problem at all, obviously, in believing that it was entirely possible for the dead to come back), I say to the photos, *I know we gave away most of your clothes but I have a lot of your nice sweaters and scarves and I think some of your coats might still even be in the coat closet at Dad's and I will of course give you all the jewelry back and I will give you your car back and all the money so that you can go buy whatever else you need and if you would just come back even for five minutes so I could ask you a bunch of stuff I forgot, I would pretty much do anything,* and so with regard to my showing some kind of feelings nonverbally to Joe I was pretty much thinking, *Well what's the point really? So I can have a long-term commitment with another photo?*

I didn't hear from Joe for a while, and I was pretty sure he'd given up until one day the doorbell rang while I was taking a bath; Christina was listening to Lenny Kravitz and dancing a little. I hadn't been counting on anyone coming to the door, much less that Christina would answer it, and I don't know how she did it, but she got herself up on a chair and finagled that doorknob and there was Joe, no doubt more than a little surprised to see a ghost baby standing there and no one else. I got out of the tub and was reaching for my robe when I heard the door open and I heard Christina saying, *Come on in,* and since he didn't run screaming into the street, I guess he wasn't as freaked out as I imagined he would be, and the next thing I knew, there they were in my living room, dancing to "Fly Away." I burst into tears immediately, and Joe took me by the hand and spun me around and we all wiggled our hips and waved our hands in the air, solemnly.

Proposal

IT SEEMS SO DUMB NOW. It seems like this day and my dumbass love life are irrelevant under the circumstances, it seems like the fact that most years I'm single on this day and that the years when I'm not single on this day have been — well, not a lot better than the years when I wasn't, sometimes inarguably worse, it seems dumb, it seems super lame, like, *Who cares?* It seems like I should be thinking about something more important, like volunteering, like giving blood, like *enlisting*, like I should convince whoever's in charge to let me enlist even though I'm too old and I've never even worked out, you know, ever, and would probably be sent to the infirmary on day one after the third push-up. Half the people I know already understood this day to universally suck, and I don't think that's different now — no, I take that back, I think it is different now, I think it sucks more. I think it sucks more now, and I'll tell you why it sucks more, this is why, for the same reason that Mother's Day sucks for me, for the same reason that Father's Day sucks for my friend Jane, because we no longer have a Mother or a Father, because we are assaulted on these days with greeting-card commercials and human-interest stories and dinner specials and catalogs for gifts we can't give anymore, and so although this day ordinarily sucks for me on what now seems like this super lame level, what I'm trying to say is that this day, for years to come now, is going to suck more because a huge number of people suddenly lost their boyfriends, girlfriends, fiancées, spouses, life partners. You can imagine that February 14 sucks now for a lot of these people where it probably didn't ever suck, or that it once sucked and then they forgot that it sucked, or maybe even a few of them remembered how much it sucked and were really really grateful when it finally didn't suck, that what used to be a day of chocolate and champagne and roses and proposals and Vegas weddings is now a day to remind them of their grief, a day where they might otherwise have had moments when they smiled, or chuckled, or forgot for five or ten minutes or stopped feeling guilty about going to a movie but then were reminded of their grief, like, Oh right, Valentine's Day, my wife died, I almost forgot. So I want to propose that since Valentine's Day now sucks on multiple levels that we scrap this day altogether and call it something else and make it about something else, something more important, Memorial Day is taken and Grief Day is too depressing, so maybe something like a day about friends, something like Friends Day, I know, corny right? but whatever, that's what I think. Maybe there's already a Friends Day, I don't know, if there is it's obviously not that popular, but if there already is a Friends Day I propose it gets moved to February 14 because we all have friends, right? and even if we've lost friends, which many of us have, even if we've lost friends, we surely have other friends, right? and we could take the day to appreciate these friends, we could remember our lost friends, but not in a sad way, and not in a cheesy way, maybe there could be a rule that if you were going to send a card on Friends Day it would have to be a card that you made, to avoid the obvious pitfall that Valentine's Day has suffered over the years, the cheap dime-store cards and the whole obligation aspect of it, which is also super lame if you ask me. So that is my proposal, that we take this day and call up our people, and we send them cards that we made out of whatever, and we tell them things, we can just say, Hey, hey, you, if we can't think of anything else, or if we are not the type of people to tell our friends we love them, you know, openly. Or we can even go ahead and tell them cheesy things if we are the type of people who like cheesy things as long as we make up the cheesy things ourselves, we can tell them why we're glad they're alive and tell them to call us tomorrow and say they're okay. Because otherwise my best hope is that years from now, when these people who have lost people meet new people, when they get new valentines and new champagne and roses and proposals and Vegas weddings, that this day will at best rise to the level of bittersweet.

An Intervention

LAST THURSDAY I came home and a half dozen of my closest friends and family members were sitting around my living room looking very serious like someone had died and since I'm a little bit psychic I knew right away what was going on. It was an intervention.

Alice, said my best friend Jolie, *we are here because we care about you.*

We have all been talking, said my dad, *and we can no longer pretend that we don't see what's going on.*

We want you to know, said my therapist, *that we all have your best interest at heart, and that we will help you through this in any way we can.*

Alice, said my friend Adam, *you are not an alcoholic.*

I realized this wasn't usually the way these things went. I had seen *Sarah T.: Portrait of a Teenage Alcoholic*, the movie-of-the-week starring Linda Blair as a very bad alcoholic girl in the suburbs. But I've been a member of Alcoholics Anonymous for nearly ten years, and I'm not in denial. It's where I belong. The only requirement for membership is a desire to stop drinking; I have that. And frankly, some of those people intervening, they could stand to join up too. Let me go back.

Ten years ago I was in what stands as the worst relationship among the mostly very bad relationships I've had. This particular guy was almost twenty years older than me, a sort of minor movie star, well past the prime of his minor movie stardom, who bore little resemblance to the good-looking young actor I'd admired in some independent movies I'd seen when I was in high school. Plus, although he had been sober for several years at that point, there was clearly something really wrong with him mentally. Partly he was your basic abusive/angry guy, kind of a stalker (not my thing really, although I stand by the worst-relationship claim, against my own record) and even though there were things he was angry about (*Cars*, he'd say, *there are too many cars on the street. I can't live like this anymore.*), when he'd tell his life story it didn't seem so bad. He'd say, *You'd like my parents, everyone does*, and he'd talk about them and it didn't sound like they were any more strange than anyone's parents, maybe less so. Which got me started on thinking about him having some actual mental problem, besides alcoholism, I mean, because it seemed like that chip was missing that most people with ordinary problems have who know in even the vaguest way that their problems are not someone else's fault. Or you know, that even if they are it's still their problem to deal with. Plus a lot of the time he'd say stuff that just didn't make sense, but you knew he really thought it did, and that he was sharing some big life truth with you that was the equivalent of "New York City is essentially run by a big blue horse." You know, nodding and winking a lot. It was possible that he was a compulsive liar, but I had no way of confirming a lot of stuff he said. (I understood that New York was not run by a big blue horse, but I was never sure if he believed it or if it was his sense of humor or, like I said, if he was a liar.) Anyway, if I'd bothered to mention it to anyone, they might have advised me against going out with someone whose picture had been on the front page of the *Daily News* for hitting his ex-wife, and it's not that I didn't take that into consideration, believe me. He had been asking me out for months already. I worked for his agent, and he started asking me out over the phone long before we ever actually met, and I'd heard about him even before the *News* thing, and like I said, he didn't really meet the criteria of Bad Boyfriend I was used to (charming and funny and exceptionally bright and noncommittal but somehow making it seem like they *were* committal even though it was still really obvious always that they weren't). He was pretty nice on the phone, but I sincerely just wasn't interested. He'd ask me out and I'd say no and he'd call back later and ask me things like, *Would you go out with me if I weren't fat?* and I'd say, *No,* and he'd ask me out again the next day and I'd say no again. I can't say I didn't like it at all, the attention, but I had other things on my mind, like how much and in what way my life sucked. It just kind of happened that he stopped by the office one day to pick up a script and I passed him by the reception desk on my way to the bathroom and in addition to really having to pee, it had been an especially bad morning at work, phones ringing off the hook because my recently promoted twenty-four-year-old boss had made some mistake on someone's contract like he always did and tried to blame it on me since I was the one who typed up the contract, except it wasn't a typo, he had forgotten to negotiate for a double-wide trailer for one of his bigger clients and when she got to the set she was super freaked out about why her costar had a double-wide and why did she have to languish in a single-wide and there was no way my boss would ever take the blame for that kind of thing. (I tried once, very diplomatically, to point out evidence of an earlier mistake, and he said, *I'm an agent and you're not*, which, you know, what do you say to that, really?) Not to mention that a double-wide trailer would have been a vast improvement over the apartment I was living in at the time, and my patience was growing a little thin about this kind of thing.

So in a rush to pee and get this guy off my back, I agreed to go to a movie with him later (*Fine*, I think was my response) and he called about four more times to confirm, and the last time he called he asked if it was okay if his nieces (who happened to be in town) came along and I was thinking, Oh how cute, that they'd be like, eight or something, but they were college students, and they *were* cute, but in an eighteen-year-old way, and they came on our date with us, and I never really did find out if they were just — more dates or something. Backup. We went to a midnight show of *JFK* at the Paramount, and it was actually kind of crowded for a midnight showing of a three-hour movie, and Jake couldn't find a seat he liked, and we moved about three times before he was satisfied, and between the "nieces" and the moving it wasn't the best of dates even for me, and by the time the movie was over the temperature outside had dropped to about four degrees, and it was three-thirty in the morning and I could think of nothing I'd ever wanted more than to be under my covers, in my bed, alone, and I was certain that my eagerness to get home would be apparent enough to my date that he would see no reason to call me again. It did finally occur to me that the girls probably *were* nieces, because they very graciously offered to get in a separate cab and leave us alone, but I was just like, *Not necessary.* So then I did go home to bed and slept in because the next day was Saturday and Jake called around eleven to tell me I was a really a good sport about the nieces and the seat-moving and he'd really like to go out with me again. Which I found to be completely baffling, but he wouldn't let me off the phone until I agreed to a second date, and by then I just didn't have it in me to fight anymore, and assumed that sooner or later we'd end up getting married because I'd be too exhausted to argue about it. Plus also, really, at this point, and this is the part that is supposed to somehow tie into how I ended up in Alcoholics Anonymous, I just thought, this is the best I'll ever do.

So we went out again, and no one came with us on our second date, and he brought me a little bunch of wilted flowers, which I have to say a lot of my other bad boyfriends never did, although having seen all the talk shows I did already know that abusive stalking boyfriends were like that, saying really nice things and bringing flowers and on alternate days channeling evil aliens and making the front page of the *News*. On this particular date, though, Jake took me to a Texas kind of place I really liked, and I didn't so much mind that he was eating with his hands — he had ordered fried chicken, but it was like his napkin wasn't even there, and the grease was all over his hands and his chin and it didn't seem to bother him at all or concern him that this would detract from the preexisting slim chance that I would ever kiss him, which was very far from my mind from the beginning. I just didn't want to. And again, the question of his possibly being a compulsive liar came up, because he started telling me that he loved me, on the second date, but he'd say it with a sort of smirk and then take another bite of chicken, and then with a mouthful of chicken he'd say, *But then again I'm really gay, so it probably won't work out.* And you know, this not being really funny, it was hard to say if this was just his sense of humor or what.

I somehow managed to avoid kissing Jake for a few weeks; I just didn't want to, and it was actually a sort of inadvertent lesson in that thing I guess some women do that makes men like them more, except it didn't carry over into any of my other relationships, because if I want to kiss someone I just do, I can't just not kiss them because of some plan. In fact, generally things happen extremely quickly with me, because if I really like someone I really like them and I sort of just know they're going to be my boyfriend for a few months (the psychic thing) and if I don't really like them I won't even go on a date with them. I just think, what's the point of that? He didn't complain about it and didn't even ask about it for weeks; I'd say maybe he was used to it except there's always someone who will sleep with a celebrity, no matter what kind of mental problems they have.

Then it was Valentine's Day and he gave me this big valentine like the kind you make in grammar school, with a big doily, and candy hearts glued on it and a poem, "Roses are red, violets are blue, I know I said I was gay, but I like you," and he brought me a bag of cookies, even though he had chocolate on his fingers and I knew he'd eaten one on the way to my house, and I figured it would be ridiculous not to kiss him at this point, even though it still wasn't anything I had any compulsion to do, and then the actual kiss was kind of unmemorable, and a little chocolatey, but he didn't try to have sex with me or anything, which made me wonder if he really *was* gay, except that he had kids by about four different women and was stalking at least two of them. Then one time after that I went over to his apartment, which was remarkably nicely decorated in a totally girly kind of way (it kinda looked like *my* house), which I point out not to say that it made me think he was any more gay, just that I saw the overstuffed couch and a couple of cool flea market items and found it endearing that he had a real homey kind of decor. Unfortunately, we were kissing and it still really didn't do anything to make me want to have sex with him, and something possessed me to bite his lip, which he got kind of mad about. It wasn't a playful bite. He had a right to be mad, but in the middle of kissing him I saw this stack of valentines, and a bottle of glue and the candy hearts and I was a little bit jealous and mad myself. Which is inexplicable, really, because I never had any romantic feelings for him, but I thought he should have romantic feelings only for me. I went home and I was again figuring, Oh he just won't call me, and I'd get out of the whole thing without having to break up with him, but that wasn't what happened. I only lived right around the corner but when I got home he'd already left me two messages apologizing and saying that he wasn't serious with any of those other girls like he was with me and not to forget that he really liked guys anyway. I told him to stop calling me and he kept calling back until I relented again and agreed to be his girlfriend. He said he'd break up with all his other girlfriends which I didn't know if it was a joke or what, and I was just like, *Fine*, again, *let me get some sleep now.*

Then, to what I thought was about to be my great relief, he went off to do a movie in Chicago, which I thought would give him a chance to find some other girl to bother, except it didn't, he called me at work from the plane, *from the plane,* and what happened instead of my being relieved of him was that some little part of me started to like him just then, which if you think about it I should have known would be the easiest way to get rid of him, except what I was hoping was that I could somehow break up with him both without pain and without breaking up with him. Nobody ever called me from the plane before. He called me from the plane to ask me to come visit him in Chicago.

So I did, I made a reservation (and if there's any remaining question about Jake having mental problems, he was almost dumbfounded that I was able to phone the airlines entirely on my own, which apparently he was incapable of doing, like it was a disorder or something) and I flew to Chicago, stayed with him in his room at the Drake (another thing he saw fit to be angry about, *wasteful* he called it, even though he wasn't paying for it) and sure enough he was mostly really mean to me, telling me what to wear, going out without me I don't know where and coming back really late, explaining my whole life to me in some kind of bizarre language I couldn't interpret (*You don't act,* he'd say, *you re-act.*) and blaming the bad sex on me, which I'm sorry, it was totally not my fault that I couldn't breathe (and therefore couldn't move to even try to satisfy him) because he was crushing me. We fought the whole time and I was about to change my reservation when he took me to an "open" meeting of Alcoholics Anonymous, which means that friends and family members of alcoholics can come and I guess understand. And what I came to understand at this meeting of A.A., was that *I* was an alcoholic, that everything that was wrong with me was because I was an alcoholic. All those things that made no sense to me suddenly made sense, and when they said, *Not to embarrass you but to welcome you, is this anyone's first meeting of Alcoholics Anonymous,* I raised my hand and I said, *My name is Alice and I'm an alcoholic,* and people were clapping, like I'd done something really fantastic; they said, *You are the most important person here,* which I didn't question, and afterward they kind of swarmed me, and handed me coins, these coins they give out in commemoration of the accomplishment of not drinking for a day, and I belonged somewhere. I was the most important person somewhere.

Unfortunately, I didn't live in Chicago at the time, and I didn't have any way of knowing if my importance in Alcoholics Anonymous there would carry over to New York, but it did, and I heard more and more people saying things I understood, about not fitting in, and having bad relationships and problems with money and stuff. Of course there was also a lot of talk about drinking, and how they couldn't stop on their own, no matter how hard they tried, and all the bad things that happened, car accidents, jail and all, and I didn't really have any stories like that because I'd only been drunk one time. A few weeks after I got to college I went to the campus bar with some people from the dorm and had seven apricot brandy sours in a couple of hours and became very drunk, and liked it very much, and not having ever been drunk before I thought for sure I must be an alcoholic if I liked it so much, and so I quit on the basis of willpower. But they tell you, especially if you go to beginners meetings, to identify with the feelings, and not the facts, and I very much did identify with the feelings. Plus there were so many cute guys it was unbelievable, and that got me to do what they call a ninety and ninety, which means you go to ninety meetings in ninety days, which wasn't any problem for me since by this time I'd left my horrible job and was unemployed.

The other miraculous thing was that all these great things started happening almost immediately; without even trying, I fell in with what I was sure was the coolest bunch of people, who were artsy but not pretentious, mostly actors, mostly very cute guys. (There are suggestions in A.A., one of which is that the women stick with the women and the men with the men, when you're new, and there were a couple of women in the group so that it didn't look so bad that I was hanging out with a lot of guys, but there were times when I went for coffee after the meeting and it was me and like, eight mostly really cute guys and, frankly, a lot of people didn't follow that suggestion so I didn't feel all that bad about it.) And I mean, I was telling all these people the total truth about my drinking story, and not one of them told me I was in the wrong place. I would describe the feelings I had, before, during, and after the drinking, about how I felt uncomfortable around people, and how that time when I drank I felt exhilarated, how it seemed so stupid that I hadn't figured it out before, that a few drinks could make you feel like a debutante, and how remorseful I felt afterward. Okay, a lot of people told me I was in denial. I'd share my story and someone would come up to me after the meeting and say, *Keep coming back*, kind of sarcastically, like I'd remember the real story sometime when the fog lifted. But mostly, the people I liked, the people I made friends with, they totally understood, and they said it's not about how much you drank, it's about why you drank, and that anyone who's stopping to wonder if they're an alcoholic is usually an alcoholic.

In New York A.A., at most meetings the chairperson asks if anyone is counting days, and if you have been sober for less than ninety days, you can raise your hand every day and say, *I have thirty-five days, thirty-six days*, however many you have, and what happens is that everyone claps and cheers and whistles, every day for the ninety days, and also, in New York the meetings are mostly pretty big, so you end up having a couple hundred people cheering for you and who wouldn't love that? Then, after you get ninety days, you get to qualify, if someone asks you, which means you get to be the speaker and tell your drinking story. I have no problem talking about myself and wasn't the least bit worried about telling my story, and I know I talked for too long that first time, which you find out later is not uncommon for newly sober people. I felt like if I explained everything about my life leading up to the time I got drunk, along with everything after up until the time I came to Alcoholics Anonymous, and how it was just miraculous that I was able to feel the belonging, that I had this fantastic group of new friends I'd never had before, that people would really understand, which they did, because a lot of them came up to me afterward and said it was a great qualification and they totally identified and said they also had *high bottoms* which is not what it might sound like but means actually that you quit drinking before things got totally out of control. *You don't have to take the elevator all the way to the basement,* was what people told me in reassurance that I belonged.

Jake and I had a typical sort of nonbreakup right after I got into the rooms of A.A. I didn't get a big explanation and I was a little upset that he didn't want to share the experience of sobriety with me, but I think he was following the suggestion of not getting involved with newcomers, even though we were previously involved and I don't think that's the rule. I got over it pretty fast because before the end of my first six months I started to have a big crush on a guy named Brian, who was having his first anniversary at the time. We started out just being really good friends, and we talked about everything but a lot about god, who he seemed to know for sure was looking after me even though I was never so sure, and I liked that he believed that. *If you're having trouble seeing god,* he said, *just look in the mirror,* which made me just about weep, and by the time we slept together he had a year and he said it was okay that we didn't follow the suggestion because for a newcomer, I was very advanced in the program of Alcoholics Anonymous. I was very upset of course when he came over all dressed up a few weeks after we started sleeping together, asking if he could borrow fifteen dollars because I totally knew due to my being slightly psychic that he was on his way to a date (forget that it's hard to imagine where he was going to go on his fifteen-dollar date in New York City), and I was of course kind of miffed that he'd come try to borrow fifteen dollars from me to go on a date with someone else. But I do have to say, overall I felt that my experience with Brian was a positive one because of certain things that took place sexually that I had never really enjoyed before, which I attributed to my sobriety and my ability to experience the feelings of satisfaction that I had previously not allowed myself to have. So I don't really have regrets about that.

Plus right after that I got this amazing job. I was thinking about becoming a teacher, and one day I was flipping channels and I landed on a talk show just as this guy was on saying he was a tutor to kids in the movies, and I felt it was a sign that I should do that, and I mentioned it to one connected person that I knew and about five minutes later I was on an airplane to Massachusetts to work on a movie. It happened so easily and quickly that it was clear that it came about because of my having joined Alcoholics Anonymous and my new openness to seeing signs. Also I was feeling much better about myself as a result of the joining, and I believe that came across to the people who hired me. So I flew up to Massachusetts and there I was having my own double-wide trailer! It was the schoolroom. I had a hotel room. But I did think it was a little ironic, because I had a lot of lounging time while my student was doing scenes, and it might as well have been mine. Anyway, I went to some A.A. meetings up there but it was a pretty small town so the meetings were like, me and six of the Gorton's fishermen, and actually they were the only ones I've ever run into who thought I wasn't an alcoholic, before the intervention. They looked at me and said things like, *You're not really one of us*, and, *I spilled more than you drank*, which of course was entirely possible, even though it didn't matter to me. I even related to the Gorton's fishermen.

Then to celebrate my first anniversary I had a little party and all of the cute guys came, and the two other girls, and my friend Michael gave me his one-year coin, which had been given to him by his sponsor, and my friend Jason brought me flowers, and Brian brought me a beautiful card which I felt to be a sincere gesture of friendship even though he was totally in love with the fifteen-dollar girl. Michael stood up and stopped everyone from their conversations for a minute and said, *I just want to tell everyone here that I love them very much*, and I know it was my party and everything, but at first I thought he was just being nice, that there was no way he could have been meaning to include me in that, except for he was almost weeping, and I was moved so far as to actually believe he did have that kind of love for all of us. Everyone else was used to it I guess because they were just like, *Yeah, we love you too, Mikey, sit down*, but I was not used to emotive displays of this sort, and I believe it contributed greatly to the building of my self-esteem. Jason and Michael stayed after everyone else left to watch a movie, and when Michael got up to go to the bathroom, Jason started kissing my neck, which was enjoyable and he too was very cute but I had no idea he was interested in me that way, and Michael was right in the bathroom, so I made him stop, and then the next time I saw him after that at a meeting I asked him what that was all about and he said he had no idea what I was talking about, that it had never happened. I didn't know if he had lost some brain cells in his alcoholic experience, but it did happen. That's a very strange thing, when someone says something didn't happen and you know it did. There's no argument, or there's a very never-ending argument, and I didn't see the point of that so I let it go, and then one day we were at the movies, and not a particularly sexy movie at that, in fact it reminded me a little of Jake because the main character was this kind of abusive/angry father, but then suddenly in the movies Jason had his hand on my thigh, in a high location, and we didn't end up seeing the rest of the movie, really, and then we were the kind of buddies who have sex for a while, although we also talked about god, which made it seem a lot less awful to me, and plus also I learned that my enjoyment with Brian wasn't just a fluke. But then one time we were fooling around in Jason's roommate's bed and something scratched me in the back and it was his roommate's retainer and I thought, Well, maybe it could be better than this. Which was also a lesson in sobriety to me because previously I was of the mind, you might re-

call, that it couldn't be better than Jake, which, looking back, or if you are someone else, you might think
was obviously not true, but if you had been me before
I joined Alcoholics Anonymous, you wouldn't have
known that.

Shortly after my second anniversary of sobriety, I
was hired by the same family to tutor some of their
other kids (they had a lot, which was good for me) on
another movie, in Chicago. I wasn't all that excited
really because I was still feeling so "a part of," which
in A.A. just means the same as what it would mean if
you left on the word *something* at the end, and it was
going to be a long shoot, but I needed the work, so I
went. My hotel room had a kitchen and a fantastic
view of Lake Michigan, which helped, but I ran up a
hundred-dollar long-distance bill in the first three days
I was there. (Although, curiously to me at the time, I
did feel a very strong connection with my midwest-
ern roots, and I had always liked Chicago. I felt very
much at home there, which I didn't tend to feel much
of anywhere, least of all in my hometown of New
York, in spite of the recent belonging.) I knew a few
people from the crew of the last movie, and one of the
other teachers had heard about this hip neighborhood
called Wicker Park, so we got in a cab and went there
only to find nothing but a grungy-looking coffee shop
on Division Street, and I was not very comfortable in

this neighborhood that for some reason reminded me of parts of Mexico City I'd passed through, and we'd just gotten paid so I had all of my per diem in my pocket, which was several hundreds of dollars (several hundred more than I would normally ever have, or carry), and I was not at all sure what was so hip that was going on there that I should overlook the feelings of endangerment I was experiencing.

I figured it out quickly, though, when our waiter came over and he was wearing a very Seattle worn-flannel kind of outfit, torn dungarees and long johns, and his hair, in a ponytail, was longer than even mine was at the time, and he had one of those goatee beards that doesn't have a mustache, which on any but the cutest guys makes them look like a leprechaun, and this guy did not lean to the leprechaun side in any way, and I was pretty sure the waiters in Chicago weren't all actors, that maybe he was just a waiter, or in a rock band. Anyway, he was very cute, and very hip, his name was Steven, and I decided that he would be my boyfriend, and I went back a couple of days later to ask him out for coffee and he said yes, and then he called sooner than he even said he'd call, and asked if I wanted to go to dinner, which of course I did. He picked me up at my hotel room very dressed up, which I had not expected, wearing actual pants, and a white shirt, and a vest and a jacket, and his hair was loose and all brushed, and it turned out that it was the first time he'd had a trim in four years, which I thought was kind of sweet, and he had flowers, a bunch of wildflowers, not wilted. I was just wearing jeans and a cardigan, having hardly expected the Seattle guy to be looking so fancy, but it was fine, really, and he took me to a very hip new restaurant in the meat-packing district, which was on the expensive side, and it was for sure the best most fancy date I'd ever had. Plus I was really surprised at how cool Chicago was, and I was thinking right away that if he gave me a good reason I'd move there in about three seconds.

He asked if I wanted to order a bottle of wine, but I said I didn't drink, and he asked me about it, so I told him that I was a member of Alcoholics Anonymous, and he asked if I minded if he drank, which I didn't, so he ordered a scotch and had a couple more before the end of the night, but he never seemed drunk to me at all. He asked me a few questions about being in A.A. but not so many that it was weird at all, and then he told me this story about how one time he was on a date with this girl and they were driving around looking for a restaurant and ended up sitting down at what they first thought was an outdoor café but later realized (when they asked the people at the table next to them for a menu, to quite a bit of laughter) was really just some tables set up outside of a church basement where they were having an A.A. meeting, which they also thought was funny, and even more funny when she later did end up going to A.A. not accidentally but because of a drinking problem. (Although I did file this anecdote away mentally, because in A.A. it's said that no one gets there by accident, even though a lot of people who end up there have similarly amusing anecdotes.) He never asked me about A.A. after that, really, which was fine, and we had things to talk about, and the restaurant was closing so we went to this bar where he also works called Dr. Bob's, which he's also part owner of and which I should also say went into my mental notes because Dr. Bob is the name of the co-founder of Alcoholics Anonymous.

He asked me if I wanted to have kids. On the first date. You know, that's the thing we're not supposed to bring up on any date, ever. He said he very much wanted to have kids one day. We talked a lot about our families, and I gathered his wasn't any more normal than mine, and we ended up talking until around two A.M., which was very late for me although not for him, because he told me the next day he actually went back to Dr. Bob's after he dropped me off, which I didn't think much of because he said he was wide awake from having had such a great time on his date with me, and that he wanted to see me again as soon as possible, which I thought was very sweet. He had theater tickets and seemed almost shy about asking me out again, which seemed crazy to me, because he was totally cute and it was hard to believe he didn't have lots of girlfriends, but anyway, I was in love already, and either my psychic abilities weren't working or he was really different from all the previous bad boyfriends, that he was by all appearances going to be a good boyfriend. I must admit to having had some trepidations, having been so used to bad boyfriends, and there's a certain thing about having bad boyfriends whereby it's just not that big of a disappointment if you break up with them, and I had some concerns about what it would be like to break up with someone I was in such instantaneous true love with, now that I was becoming more in touch with my feelings as a result of having quit drinking. (They tell you in A.A. that your feelings are a gift, and it's not like you don't get the point, but on the other hand, sometimes it doesn't seem so true, and you look the horse bringing that particular gift directly in the mouth and say, *No thank you to that, gift horse.*) Anyway, it was a risk I was willing to take, and I would say for that first month I was absolutely certain that I was going to move to Chicago and spend the rest of my life with him.

He said the nicest things. Things I had never in my life heard before. On the second date he asked me if anyone ever asked me to marry them, and I said, *Um, no,* and he said he found that astonishing, and he asked me how I felt about Wednesday, and I thought he was meaning if I was available for a date the next Wednesday, and he said, *No, I mean about our date* (which had been on the last Wednesday), and I didn't think there was any doubt that I was madly in love, so I was kinda like, *Are you kidding?* and he said that he had felt like he was in a bubble, that if I hadn't pointed out that the waiters were putting the chairs on the tables and mopping the floors, that he could have just stayed there and talked to me forever. Forever.

I somehow managed to not sleep with him until the third date, but it didn't really matter. I was in love. He wore those kind of long Calvin Klein underwear, which seemed uncharacteristic given the Seattle thing he had going on, but they looked totally sexy on him. The sex was great and I felt that my continued satisfaction in that area was indicative of my growing emotional progress.

It went like this for a month. Day after day he called when he said he'd call, and said things I'd never heard before. He said, *I like you, Alice. I'd rather be with you than just about anywhere.* He remembered that I don't like nuts with my sweets. He carried around the notes I left him when I went to work in the morning, that just said like, "That was fun, make yourself some coffee if you want." I met his friends. That was maybe the first bad sign, though. I felt a little different. They had tattoos. (I wanted one tattoo, but these were, you know, tattoo people. Purple hair. Facial piercings. This one guy seriously had a bone through his nose. And he was actually pretty nice to me, I'm not saying anything about what kind of people they were, just that I was back to that thing of feeling totally not cool.) Steven didn't even have a tattoo, which I thought he was a ripe candidate for, and he said he'd thought about it but he was Jewish and was worried about what his parents would think, which did not at all seem characteristic due to his having long hair and an earring and a general attitude of rebellion. I think his friends liked me fine, because one of them once told him right while I was standing there that if Steven didn't marry me he was going to. I realize now, because of my time in the program, that feeling not a part of isn't necessarily the reality of what's going on. Feelings aren't facts, is a saying they have. But I still felt a little out of my element, even though Steven was always attentive and included me in everything.

Except for he never had me over to his apartment, which was another one of the first ways in which I felt like something wasn't quite right, even though he swore that the only reason was that it was more his dogs' apartment than his, and that it smelled like pit bull no matter what he did, and I couldn't reassure him that I didn't care, and so I never saw it even one time. I made one more mental note, though, the one time I met him in front of his apartment, because it was the first time in my entire life I had ever heard gunshots, which some people might think was surprising due to my having lived in New York my whole life, but you know, I didn't grow up in the South Bronx. I was standing out there waiting for him to come down and he shouted out the window that he'd be right there, and right when he opened the door I heard these popping sounds, *so* not like it sounds in the movies, but still, even when you haven't ever heard gunshots before, you have a pretty good idea what it is, and I said, *Okay, what was that?* and he said very casually, *Oh, the little bangers are having some fun,* like it was funny to him, like he was totally used to it, which I'm sure he was, because he told me he came home one time and there was a bullet hole in his window and a shell on his bed, and he lives on the second floor. So I was like, okay, note to self, when you move to Chicago, don't live here, which would later be ironic. Anyway, I also finally got the nerve to ask him why he wore a wedding band. I knew he wasn't married, he told me on the first date he'd never been married, but he did say that he was very serious with this one woman and they wore rings, and I didn't want to be rude in pointing out that they had broken up a year before, but he could probably tell that's what I was thinking, and he said it was just kind of a reminder, but he never really said of what, which made me think it was a reminder of *her*, only not the mistake of her. It was obvious he'd been madly in love with her, which made me psychically know that she was a tall dark-haired supermodel, which he said she pretty much was, and I began feeling totally less than, which is another thing they say in A.A. that leaves off the end of the sentence, meaning less important than fill-in-the-blank, it could be anything or anyone you think is better than you or you think someone thinks is better than you, which for me is often everything and everyone, which I found out in A.A. is very alcoholic. This supermodel was described to me as being a very strong person, which I would in the course of his sad tale of heartbreak discover really meant she had a strong personality, because in fact, this girl had partly gone out with Steven because she couldn't leave her last relationship, and I learned that she had broken a lot of hearts up to and including his, when she finally cheated on him in the end with little remorse.

And so I went to a lot of extra meetings, because even though I was still very much in love I was feeling increasingly anxious, like the reality was somewhere in my mind that Steven would realize that he'd made a terrible mistake in dating outside of his cool habitat. Anyway, at one of the meetings they read the promises, which is this passage from the Big Book of Alcoholics Anonymous in which it lists all these great things that will happen to you if you practice the steps, which includes a lot of things that I was always hoping for, like, "We will comprehend the word serenity and we will know peace," and "We will see how our experience can benefit others," and "That feeling of uselessness and self-pity will disappear," and also "Fear of economic insecurity will leave us," and also "We will suddenly realize that God is doing for us what we could not do for ourselves," and I realized that some of those things were happening, that although I was not totally experiencing the serenity, I did feel more useful to the world and somewhat less self-pitying and I was definitely feeling economically secure, and it caused me to realize that if some of the promises were coming true that maybe more of them would come true later, and that was an especially profound realization even though I'd heard the promises a hundred times by then.

But then I went to another meeting and shared that I was dating this guy and I was scared because I really liked him, and at first there was a lot of nodding, like they understood my feelings of fear but then when I mentioned that he owned a bar, not at all trying to make any point of that, they actually crosstalked to me. As a group, everyone in the room suddenly said, *He owns a bar?* Which I took to mean that I was remiss in my not realizing that that was some big problem, for which one of us I didn't know, but which was not how I saw it anyway, and the thing is, the rule against cross-talk is like the whole reason people come to Alcoholics Anonymous, that you can say absolutely anything you want and feel safe knowing that no one is going to make any judgmental comments like your family or your friends or your bosses do. And then everyone laughed (except for me), because they undoubtedly surprised themselves as much as they surprised me, albeit in their case because it was an unplanned group cross-talk. It was upsetting.

Steven was still very much in my life but I started to notice a lot of things that usually I pick up psychically on the first date, things that don't bode well for the future together that I initially had envisioned. I started to figure out that he had his own weird rule system of life, like if things in the law didn't make sense to him, he went around it and did not seem to have any worries about it whatsoever, whereas I am a person who has been worrying very much about going to jail ever since I didn't return *Old Yeller* to the New York Public Library in 1971. He got parking tickets outside of my hotel room almost every single day and would just toss them in the back seat, and he also hadn't had a valid driver's license for several years, so his idea was that he would just drive very cautiously, and also he had this other thing where he only drove really old bad cars and when one would get to the point where it would just not go, he would leave it wherever it was and take off the plates and get a new old bad car (which was also kind of his philosophy of clothes; rather than doing laundry he would just buy a huge lot of thrift-store clothing and eventually get rid of it after meaning to wash it but then not) and he was a miraculously lucky person that way, because it worked.

Plus also there was a certain point in the relationship where I felt like the conversation was turning largely to cars and dogs, all the time, and I didn't really have so much to say about cars, and although I love dogs, it's not a sustainable main topic of conversation for most people who aren't dog breeders (an aspiration of his). I'd also like to add that Steven had an idea that he was qualified to do some kind of home veterinary medicine, which was kind of disturbing to me. He would give me these graphic descriptions of how he fixed torn ears and tails after the dogs got into a fight, and he was obviously very pleased with himself, and I didn't really want to take that away from him, and probably at that point I was more upset about the downturn in conversation than I was about his home veterinary practice. But it just kept piling up, all the things that were making me feel like he was going to break up with me eventually, and because I was keeping late hours but still going to work in the morning I got a cold that wouldn't really go away.

And also, Steven, though he was totally not like

Jake, would very casually say that he made out with some guy friend of his at Dr. Bob's, I guess just to be funny or open or it was some type of cool ritual I never understood, because (a) the only guys I knew who made out with guys were gay or bisexual and (b) even if he was bisexual, he was still with me. But he didn't see it as anything, and I think it bothered him that I did. And then there was one really warm night in the spring when he came over to the lake with all of his friends after the bar closed, and they were all passing around a joint, which made me feel like I was back in high school saying, *No thanks, I'm good,* like they would hopefully take that to mean I was already stoned when what they were probably taking it to mean was that I was good, meaning that I thought I was better than a person who would smoke pot. Anyway, on that night everyone started skinny-dipping, including Steven, and they were all just friends really, but I was experiencing some feelings of jealousy that he was letting this naked girl dive off his naked shoulders, and at that point I think something turned over in my mind finally to where I was just waiting for him to break up with me.

He didn't openly seem like he was less interested really, though, and we were still spending a lot of time together, and one day we went to the dog beach with his dog Wilbur, who was actually my favorite of the pit bulls. None of his dogs seemed mean like you know a lot of pit bulls are, but Wilbur especially was just like a big lap dog. Anyway, we were at the dog beach, and we were tossing around a Frisbee with Wilbur, and it went kind of far at one point so Wilbur ran after it and another dog got it and they got into a big dogfight, and Steven ran over there to stop him. I stayed put, having no desire to get close to a big dogfight, although I could see it perfectly well from where I was standing, and Steven got up to them and the other dog had Wilbur's ear in his mouth, like, off his head and separate from Wilbur, whose yelping was audible from where I was, and before I knew it Steven took out a handgun I can assure you I had no idea was on his person and shot Wilbur in the head and he went down. Wilbur was dead. And I had a very sick feeling in my stomach, again, it felt like no kind of gift to me to be feeling the sickness of watching my boyfriend shoot his dog out of what I knew he would try to tell me was some kind of home veterinary humanity, and he actually was shouting something at the owner of the ear-eating dog, which in my opinion it seemed like he was pushing things somewhat because of his just having fired a handgun publicly, and I wasn't at all worried that I was in any danger of being shot by my boyfriend, but I couldn't really pretend at that point that we weren't really different then. He didn't come back over to me right away, but when he finally did he gave me money to take a cab home without saying much of anything else and that was also the first time he didn't call me for a few days, and when he finally did he didn't say one word about Wilbur and there were those long silences that happen when you just run out of things to say to a person, and it never went back the other way, although we did stay together for a few more silent weeks after that, still.

The denouement of the Steven story is that about a week before he finally did break up with me, there was a big party at Dr. Bob's, a seventies prom theme, and due to my high school being really small and/or lacking in school spirit, we didn't have a prom, which I felt was one of those American experiences I lost out on, and so it was pretty fun, picking out a cheesy (but cute, of course) light blue polyester dress which totally but accidentally went with Steven's light blue polyester tuxedo, and he brought me a corsage and everything, actually he even borrowed his dad's car, which I thought was a creative use of humor. We danced and got our photos taken, and I was forced to stay up until sunrise, on principle, and it was one of the only times I ever really questioned his possibly addictive personality traits. He told me it wasn't any big secret, but it was the first I knew that he carried around a crack pipe with him, and he didn't seem to feel uncomfortable in any way smoking crack in front of me on prom night, and I had no inclination to sample the crack, as I had preferred a more relaxing type of altered consciousness in my drinking days, but it wasn't a good sign, even though he said he never bought it himself and that I should understand I guess that he only used crack socially.

And then a week later we went to a movie but he didn't want to stay over afterward, and we had gone from talking about dogs to not talking much to talking not at all, and I knew psychically that it was over for him, I was sure because of my lack of coolness, but he wouldn't come out and just say he didn't think it was working out, it was very clear that he wanted to hand that responsibility over to me, which I had no interest in doing both because I still wanted to work it out and also I believe strongly that if you are going to break up with someone you shouldn't leave the other person to just guess about it. Not in the sort of advanced relationship where they're telling you things like, *I'm crazy about you*, no matter how short of a time it lasts. But he just wouldn't say it, for hours, until I was just like, *I have to go to bed. Just say something*, and he started to get a tear in his eye out of what I was supposed to understand was his empathy for me and not because he was really sad to lose me, and said something about things just not being right. He said that friends thing, and I said, *No I do not want to be friends with you*, which surprised me, as it flowed out of my mouth so freely, and which I felt even in my worst pain of loss was another sign of the promises coming true (the one about god doing for you what you could not do for yourself), because I had a previous tendency to stay friends with my ex-boyfriends and never get over them in a complete way, and I slammed the door and then I had to get dressed because it was morning and it was time to go to school.

The first few weeks after we broke up I have to admit I had a reversal of my gratitude about the promises coming true, mainly with regard to self-pity and uselessness taking over, and I cried almost every minute of every day and I went only to work and back to the hotel and couldn't even concentrate on a magazine, I was so singly focused on trying to discover what it was that was so fully wrong with me that I could not keep a boyfriend for more than a few months ever. I had to excuse myself from the kids several times each day to go to the bathroom because I'd feel myself starting to sob while reading *Curious George*, which, you know, isn't really the saddest reading material. I felt ruined. And I wouldn't know if anyone else had ever felt the feeling of being ruined before, but the idea is that it's not reversible, like a coffee stain on a white shirt.

But also, I didn't believe him. I thought he would come to his senses, because of his having said the things he said, which I felt couldn't just go away like that. I couldn't see how you could wonder for months how someone could not have ever been proposed to, but then later you could. I was of the mind that our love was too much of a feeling for him, and also at the end I was thinking he could possibly have a drug and alcohol dependency, but one more thing they tell us in A.A. is that the disease of alcoholism is self-diagnosed, which is sort of a polite way of saying it's not really your place to judge, but also that most alcoholics and drug addicts don't quit when it's someone else's idea. So, I wasn't really sure about that, but it was a thought in my mind that was the only thought I had that didn't involve something being wrong with me personally. I could well imagine that a drug addict would have a hard time being in a relationship with a person in the program of Alcoholics Anonymous, even if they were saying they think it's great for you.

Anyway, I just couldn't stop crying for very long until one day when my student, who was nearly eight and having a hard time learning how to read, suddenly read a word when we weren't even working on it, which we had been for months, working very hard on it, and I had a little bit of a spiritual experience then because I thought well maybe this was how I was meant to be of use. I thought maybe teaching someone to read was more important than having a boyfriend. I was so excited for him, more excited than he seemed to be, even, but it didn't feel as good as having a nice boyfriend. I won't lie. But I felt like it was maybe a beginning of trying to take care of myself again, which I had gotten so much better at before Steven, and I made a lot of phone calls and got a lot of suggestions, and I tried to learn to love myself with the use of a lot of candles and bath products, and always having flowers and just generally trying not to deprive myself of things that I subconsciously deprive myself of because I have feelings of being undeserving. It's a way of *acting as if,* again, one of those A.A. sayings that leaves off the part at the end which could be whatever, but is usually something that's an improvement over the way you would alcoholically act that theoretically leads to your being whatever it is you are only just acting like at first. I had come to believe spiritually that everything happens for a reason and believe me it was a struggle in this particular situation, but I felt that for sure Steven was a vast improvement over my past relationships and that maybe it would just slowly get better each time, and also I felt like god had given me a chance to go to the prom and maybe that's all it was.

Eventually I stopped crying on a daily basis, although to be honest I never felt like I was over Steven, even though I started dating again about a year later. I kind of went the opposite direction at first with the whole artsy/grunge/whatever thing and dated this preppy guy who liked me a lot. He was in some kind of sales,

but he chewed his fingernails all the way down to little stumps, which made me not want to have them on
me, and also I didn't think we had that much in common. I gave it a few weeks, which I thought was me
being open and willing but which maybe backfired because it gave him a chance to like me a lot and when it
became obvious that he was not going to break up
with me, I finally said something about things just
not being right, and he said, *I thought you were
everything I was looking for.* Which is among the
nicest things anyone's ever said to me, but I wasn't in
love with him or really even attracted to him. He was
just kind of regular.

I had been back in New York for a while and the
money I'd saved from Chicago was starting to run out
(it was possible that I had misinterpreted the meaning
of the promise that "fear of economic insecurity will
leave us" — I'm pretty sure I ignored the words *fear
of* because at this time I was having both actual economic insecurity and fear about it) because most of
the kids in the family I taught suddenly stopped making movies, and I went to L.A. for a while and worked
on a TV series, but I can easily skip the L.A. period because it was everything you hear about how much
L.A. sucks and worse. Some of the meetings were okay,
but there was this one meeting on the beach where
one way to be of service was to be the suntan lotion
guy, that you were to believe that if you were dis-

pensing suntan lotion at a meeting of Alcoholics Anonymous you were somehow serving god, which I just thought, I'm not saying it's not a nice thing but come on.

But I didn't want to be in New York any more than I wanted to be in L.A., although I was starting to not want to be anywhere, and then I started thinking about Chicago again, and I'm sure there were some people who thought my wanting to move to Chicago was a good example of a geographic, which means when you move somewhere because you're not happy with yourself and then nothing changes. I didn't feel like that was the case, because I felt like I had a special emotional connection with Chicago, and then I put on this Dan Fogelberg record that I seriously had not listened to in about fifteen years, and the first two songs were "Illinois" and "Part of the Plan," which I'm sorry whatever anyone thinks but it was the most clear sign I've ever gotten in my life, and I started packing my suitcases immediately, even though I didn't have a very big plan for what I was going to do after the move.

And I was packing one of my suitcases when Steven called, and I hadn't talked to him for over two years, and I couldn't believe it, and he started basically giving me a qualification over the phone and saying that he had a very bad problem with crack, and that his partners locked him out of the bar and said, *Don't come back until you're off crack.* He said they rhymed it just like that. And he asked me about Alcoholics Anonymous. And I told him about some of the meetings I'd been to in Chicago, and it came up in the course of the conversation that I was actually about to move there and he said that there was an empty apartment in his building and that he would really be grateful if I moved into it, which I interpreted every which way, and I was there twenty-four hours later sitting in an A.A. meeting with him, which I have to tell you was a rather profound moment. Between Dan Fogelberg and the phone call there was not one reservation I had about jumping on the next plane, and even though this long story is far from over, I still have not one regret about having moved to Chicago. I had strong feelings of claustrophobia in the City of New York and was unable to obtain any kind of lasting serenity there. Steven gave me the biggest apartment I'd ever lived in for not very much money, and it had a porch where I immediately planted flowers, and I felt very close to nature that way. I won't say it wasn't a little strange having him for my landlord. So there we were in that meeting and suddenly all that time later I just had the blinding revelation that the real reason Steven and I had met was so that I could help him find the rooms of Alcoholics Anonymous. It was just a lucky thing that I happened to get a great apartment out of the deal. And a few weeks after I got there I got a great job teaching preschool, which again happened with very little effort on my part but because I mentioned it to one sober person.

Although he no longer had long, flowing brown hair (which I guess was no longer cool), I of course fell in love with him all over again, within minutes, and I felt a little bit vindicated, not grateful that he had to go through crack addiction, but that there was now solid evidence that the real reason he broke up with me was because his disease was still progressing, that he did, as I suspected, have a drug and alcohol problem. There were countless moments between us during his early sobriety when I felt his loving feelings toward me, but having a few more twenty-four hours than I did when I first got into the program of A.A. I felt that I did not want to jeopardize his sobriety by even so much as talking about the romantic connection between us, even though it was very hard when he was holding my hand in his truck or standing around my doorway for too long staring at me when he dropped me off or hugging me for too long or crying on my shoulder, literally, every day for weeks, or sitting on my porch wrapped in a blanket in seventy-degree weather when I wasn't even home, or telling me that he felt like I was the only person who understood him, over and over and over again. There was no doubt that we were closer than we had ever been. I did not know, for example, the whole time we were together, that he read books. I knew he was smart but I did not know that he liked to read books. I thought he was more of the kind of mind that just remembered a lot of facts about things like why birds fly in formation (which impressed me but which I could not really contribute to). We also talked often about god, whom we had not previously discussed ever, and for a person newly off crack, he had some enlightened thoughts that had never occurred to me before. I often go back and forth in my mind about everything happening for a reason, and a lot of times it's not an enjoyable mental journey because I can see both why it would and wouldn't be true. Sometimes good things happen with such a forceful serendipity that it seems really true, but then other bad things happen that there seems to be no godly explanation for, which I'm sure is something that greater theological minds than ours had pondered but anyway not being in close touch with any great theological minds, I was in sort of a thing where I was polling people I knew (which I often did on different subjects when I did not know what to do), and when I asked him if he thought everything happened for a reason he said he guessed that he did, and he gave me what I thought was a very deep but simple explanation for why the bad things would happen, which was that we might not necessarily always know the reason. The example he gave was what if I had never met Jake? And it was true that a chain of people joining Alcoholics Anonymous formed because of my having met Jake, and that even if I hadn't moved to Chicago, Steven himself would surely have gone to meetings as a result of having met me, and that all during the bad time I was having when I was with Jake I could not have known that something very positive would come out of it. Steven's idea was that it just happened that I eventually found out the reason, but that sometimes you might not, like, some old guy could crash his car into yours and you would be very upset about having a crashed car, but maybe the old guy would suddenly realize that he should not be driving anymore, but you would have no way of knowing that. I thought it was very enlightened because I had been concentrating very hard on trying to figure things out with regard to this god thing, when maybe I didn't need to worry about it so much. Plus it's just a bonus when you can talk to any guy about god.

There were a lot of times, though, when Steven had things to say that were almost as senseless as things that Jake said, except I knew the difference was that Jake was not newly sober and a lot of times newly sober people say things that they think are startling revelations of life but again come across to anyone listening as a scrambling of sentences, which in New York A.A. they have a totally made-up word for called "mocus," the origin of which I do not know.

Jake was not mocus, and eventually, Steven was mostly not either.

It became weird, though, after a while of living in his building. We saw each other every single day, either in the building, or at a meeting, or socializing with our sober friends, many of whom we were both friends with and who did not have bones through their noses although I had the feeling that the way I felt uncomfortable around the bone people was similar to how Steven felt around most of the nonbone people. As a result of the discomfort (I thought), he showed up at my apartment one afternoon with bleached-blond hair and a bad tattoo (I thought he was having an early midlife-crisis thing due to having joined mostly nonbone people in the fellowship of Alcoholics Anonymous) that was meant to be a yin/yang symbol (him still being very much in touch with his 10 percent gay side — his words, not mine) but which, it was agreed upon by most people, looked more like a turtle, which held no particular meaning for him, saying, *You're the only one who understands me*, when the truth was even though he was right, I wasn't necessarily even telling him all my understandings about his psychological development because it wouldn't have been polite. Anyway, living in the building of your ex-boyfriend tends to foster any latent penchant for stalking inside a person, whereby if you're the sort of person who might obsess endlessly about what went wrong in a relationship but would never drive over to their house, and suddenly you're at their house all the time because it's where you live, I'm pretty sure only the very strongest person would be able to avoid looking out the window every time they heard a car door slam, or remembering the exact particular sound of someone's car starting, or interpreting the movements of the car (including nonstressful movements like times when you know he's going to work, and more emotionally testing movements like the car is not there in the morning when you go to work and trying to know that even though eight A.M. is among the times of day when he could just very well still be out from the night before, it could also be a time when he is out from the night before and sleeping at his new girlfriend's house), or knowing all the regularly parked cars on your street and when one comes that looks exactly like the one your girlfriend Sarah drives, who you remembered he said was cute that one time, and you imagine their entire secret romance and the ensuing confrontation you will have with the guy who hasn't been your boyfriend for three years. One time when he was between broken-down cars I lent him my car to go do something or other and he didn't come back until three in the morning, which I realized was probably a mistake when I remembered the time I lent Brian fifteen dollars, and I couldn't get the image of Steven and some girl kissing in my car out of my head, which I guess was not what happened anyway, but I didn't offer my car to him after that, and when he sold the building and finally moved out I was glad to be relieved of my stalking tendencies. But over time it was almost an exact duplication of our original romance with numerous boundary crossings but absolutely without any actual sexual contact for two years, during which time I stopped speaking to him at least twice in an effort to remember that he was not going to be my future husband. I cut eight inches off my hair and got a tattoo myself (of a butterfly, symbolizing transformation, and mine came out perfectly the first time).

Almost on the day of his first anniversary of being sober, Steven started dating a girl who had a bone through her forehead (at the front, between her eyebrows), and she was again tall and although she was not a supermodel I knew that in his mind she was, and I was very despondent about it. I asked him how she felt about his being 10 percent gay and he said that he wasn't 10 percent gay, that I made him say that and that his making out with a guy now and then didn't constitute a percentage of homosexuality but a sense of fun, and she was totally cool with it and that theirs was not a relationship that had to have conventional limitations anyway, although I guess I was supposed to understand that it was some kind of monogamy. I said many prayers for their greatest happiness, which is a suggestion they give you in A.A. for occasions like this when they think you are really the one with the problem and not the other people. One of the kids in my class at school was this very advanced two-year-old girl named Arabia (their language skills ranged from having 500-word vocabularies to grunting) who listened to Coltrane and woke up from a nap one day and said, *I am having the most miserable day of my life, and I will never be happy again.* I said, *I dig that, Arabia,* and we sat there on her cot nodding our heads at the floor for a while sharing the misery. She was eventually happy again and miserable again about twenty more times during the course of any given day, which you'd think might have been some kind of lesson to me but I was very much focused on obtaining an overall happiness. Anyway, it was very obvious then that I was no longer the only person Steven could talk to, because he was hardly ever calling me, and I met the girlfriend a few times and she impressed me as being way more unhappy than was even possible for me to imagine (I'm just saying that for me, it wouldn't be a celebration of my greatest joyfulness to stick something sharp into my face, and if the reverse is true among bone-wearing people, then, you know, my bad). I was figuring out that in Steven's cool world it was not very cool to be happy, and I knew that life had a lot of experiences to offer but I desired to be more happy than unhappy if at all possible and felt that I was making steady progress toward that goal. And then one day I stopped by Dr. Bob's to say hi and I had some trepidations about his girlfriend maybe being there, which she was, but on that day she engaged me in conversation and although I wouldn't have changed the unhappy impression I had of her she didn't seem as totally horrible a person as would have made it much easier for me to fully hate her, and also she was displaying some of the mocus quality I had seen in Steven earlier (even though she was not sober at all and I wouldn't have known if she was drunk, although there is some similarity between being drunk and being mocus; mocus people don't slur their words, but their meaning is just as unclear) and I thought well maybe they are really right for each other since they seem to share the mocus language, and I felt like it was a positive experience for me because I was not feeling jealous at all, and I had a few really good months of believing I was over it.

Of course Steven later broke up with her, and the very day he did that he rode his motorcycle over to my house (he had moved over from car changing to motorcycle collecting and had about a dozen of them) and came up and laid on my bed and told me his sad story, crying, asking me to help him and asking me why does he make bad choices over and over again and saying I'm the only one who understands but expecting me not to read anything into that even though it came in the same breath and it was pretty hard not to. We grew close again and he took me on a fantastic motorcycle ride by the lake, and he began to share many things with me about his feelings. He had finally come to realize his dream of dog breeding (albeit accidentally as two of his dogs, Ernestine and Cletus, who were brother and sister, got it on one time while he was out) and was very excited about it, but within a week after Ernestine gave birth to her eleven puppies she flattened all but one of them, and Steven had to put them in the freezer until he had time to take them out to the country to be properly buried, all of this causing him, in the retelling, to sob violent sobs over the memory of Wilbur and that he had been so shut down emotionally in his crack addiction that of course he could not feel the pain of that loss. Which I believed was very brave of him to admit and I felt brought us together in a new way, because I noticed that every night that he was at my house talking he was just a little bit closer to me on the couch until finally we were watching a video one time and he kissed me and I knew right then something that I had not known the first time and I don't know why I had this realization during the kiss, which was as good as it was the first time, but I knew psychically that I was going to end up being hurt even worse than the first time and yet I proceeded anyway just in case there was the smallest possibility that because of the development of his sober feelings he would be able to eventually recognize his love for me. I was also feeling a greater understanding of him on the basis of my being as addicted to him as he had been to crack, but I did not have the willingness to give him up. We didn't ever really discuss the terms of what was happening between us and I understood that there was no commitment. I just hoped.

Then what happened was something I could not have predicted, which was that while I was on a trip to New York my mother died in a very terrible accident (about which I was maybe not having so much gratitude for having worked so hard on having accessible feelings because this was a case of having many more feelings than I ever wanted to have at one time) and Steven rode his motorcycle to come to the memorial service, which I felt tremendously impressed by and I felt was not something you would do for just anyone. He was totally present for me and held my hand and rubbed my head and wiped away my tears and even though my other friends from New York were there I wouldn't have known which of them would come such a great distance to the memorial service of my mother (plus it was winter and he must have been very cold riding a motorcycle) and I felt that it was a kindness I had never known before. I stayed in New York for another week to pack up my mom's things and he went back to Chicago on his motorcycle the next day and as soon as I got back to Chicago I got a violent nauseated sickness and Steven brought me rice and ginger ale, but I knew psychically without any apparent evidence that he had gone back to the bone girl and when some apparent evidence presented itself I asked him what was going on and he admitted it. He admitted that he just happened to have run into her at a party and they talked all night and that he was in love with her even though he had previously admitted to me that the bone girl was not capable of loving feelings and was possibly in need of some medicine for her own psychiatric disorders. I was deeply saddened to have learned this a week after the tragic death of my mother and felt that although it was inevitable that our romance would find a demise that there was no reason that he had to turn a simple demise into a betrayal, and that he should have told me before my bad psychic feeling was confirmed by other sources because now he was a liar and I could never trust him again. I was not so stupid as to not realize that he knew it was a very bad time to be admitting such terrible truths, and I really didn't think he was a hateful person, but it became worse when it became a lie, and I admitted to him that I did not ever want to see him again. I was in touch with the surprising feeling of hate.

Several months after the death of my mother, when I was not leaving the house all that much, was when I came home that day to find all those people in my house telling me that they did not believe I was an alcoholic and that the program of Alcoholics Anonymous did not seem to be helping me in any way that was apparent to them and I was pretty flabbergasted but I presented all the evidence of my growth as a person and the details of my levels of feeling and they wanted to know why then was I coming home from the grocery store with my pajamas on? I pointed out that I was wearing a coat over them and it was morning and I just went to the corner to get some coffee, but because I was also wearing slippers they were not convinced. I told them that I was just taking care of myself and that I was not willing to rush my process of grief and that because of my having lost someone close to me and learning the lesson that life is short, I was no longer focusing on my love life (I learned that it was best to leave that area alone and embarked on an open-ended period of celibacy) and was instead following my lifelong secret dream of being a poet. I could tell that between the pajamas and the disarray in my house and their doubt about my alcoholism that they were formulating a B plan (contingent on my unwillingness to admit I was not an alcoholic) which was I don't know what, because there's no rehab for people who aren't alcoholics. *Just listen,* I said, and I read them this:

AN INTERVENTION

A FORCEFUL SERENDIPITY

by Alice Jones

and even though
and furthermore
and in spite of the one thing
but then also even
when she considered the other thing
and several more incidents and episodes
and maybe even because of all that
when viewing it from far away
the thing about it really
if given the choice and/or the opportunity
she was reasonably certain
she would repeat it in its entirety
with almost no changes

When
the Messenger
Is Hot

THERE IS NO EXPLANATION FOR THIS.

He is very cute, but you are thinking about other
things. You are thinking about that boy who plays
guitar that just got out of rehab. You are thinking
about that boy who graduated high school in the
nineties. You are thinking about the one you can't
have, the one you may never stop thinking about.
These are the boys that you think about. The very
fact that you use the word *boys*, at your age, says a
lot. You could make an argument for the fact that
they are all boys, these people otherwise recognized
by their age as men, but the truth is, you find yourself
more interested in men who seem like boys, ones who

work in record shops or deliver things, or who sleep really late, or who smoke as soon as they wake up, or ones who are often not even especially tall, than you are in men who seem like men, who work in offices, tall men who comb their hair and wear ties, who seem *responsible*, even though you claim to want a boyfriend who will drive. Who knows the exact location of his driver's license. Who has some kind of a vehicle. You have, in the past, considered yourself to be open-minded, you have been willing, when necessary, to do the driving, split the bill, go to a rave, but at the moment, you could be interested in a guy who drives. Who will, at least sometimes, pay.

So this cute guy starts flirting with you. He seems *happy*. You detect a little sadness around the eyes, you guess that sad things may have been seen, historically, but he seems happy. It needs to be said that he looks like a boy. He is only a little bit taller than you. He is in his thirties, but could easily pass for seventeen. He would be the perfect after-school special narc. He wears silver jewelry. He has piercings. He has tattoos. He calls them *ink*. He has fresh *ink* inside each of his wrists with the Chinese symbols for god and child. He shows them to you and says, *See, child of god*. He is committed. He is cool and happy and believes in god and he is Italian and he is from New York. You are also from New York, but you are not so cool. You exist in a cool universe but you are an impostor. You go to bed early. You have smoked maybe three cigarettes in as many decades and you have never snorted anything. You know who Chandler and Monica are.

The subject of *West Side Story* comes up. *West Side Story.* Your all-time favorite movie, the movie you'd want to have on a desert island. You say, *That is my all-time favorite movie.* He says, *Yeah?* and looks at you with heavy-lidded hazel eyes, sex eyes. *I have it on DVD,* he whispers in his New York accent. You make note that when you lived in New York, you did not find New York accents to be sexy. You make note that in Chicago, New York accents are simultaneously captivating and comforting. You make note that in Chicago, in the presence of New Yorkers with New York accents, you suddenly have a New York accent yourself. He whispers, *You wanna come over and watch it sometime?* You smile and say, *Sure.* He says, *You like fish? I could make a nice piece of fish.* You say, *I like fish.* He says, *Yeah? You like salmon? I could make you a nice piece of salmon with dill sauce?* Like a question, he says it. You say, *That sounds great.* You try to sound cool. He is now very very cute. A week ago he was just that happy guy from New York. Now you will have sex with him.

You bring dessert. You are expecting nothing. That is what you have come to expect. You quite often get more than nothing, or you get a little something and a lot of someone's *big ideas,* but never have you gotten so much more than nothing than this. You have been taken to the finest restaurants in Chicago and New York but you have never been witness to, never even heard stories of, quite such a presentation as this.

He opens the door. The lights are dim. There is music. Etta James is crooning, *At last, my love has come along, my lonely days are over . . .* There is candlelight emanating from every room in your sight. You make note that they're fancy candles, new candles. Many many brand-new fancy candles everywhere. There are fresh tulips in the living room. He shows you to the kitchen. There is a table for two set with wineglasses, placemats, more candles, *focaccia,* the works. There is something of a jungle in the kitchen. A giant, bathtub-size fish pond filled with giant fish, entirely surrounded by tropical plants. You feel like you are on an island. You smile. You are not sure, but you think your mouth may be hanging open. He smiles. He smiles a kind of Oh-it's-nothing-really smile, but you both know it's not nothing. There are pictures of babies on the refrigerator. He is someone's godfather. When you ask him about his godchild he beats his chest and says, *That's my heart.* You are a big sucker for stuff like this. You would have sex with him for the photos alone, never mind the elaborate presentation. You talk about New York and your past lives and when you tell him you're a writer he reads you his poetry and his prayers. He reads you poetry and prayers. You will not see *West Side Story*. You will have sex with him before dinner is over.

There are more fish in a tank in the living room. You comment on the tropical theme. He shows you the birds in his bedroom before he starts the movie. One bird flies out of the cage. He tells you he *hatched them from eggs*. You don't know quite what to say about this, nevertheless you are in his dimly lit bedroom talking about hatching birds from eggs. You will not see *West Side Story*. You will have sex with him right now.

It's a little chilly in the living room. He covers you both up with an afghan. Your legs are touching under the afghan. He starts the movie. He knows the dialogue. You know some of the dialogue and you know lots of *WSS* trivia and you both know all the songs. You talk and sing and giggle all through the movie and agree that there is no better movie and that possibly the clothes were better back then. He tells you he once met Gene Kelly. That he was, as a kid, a huge Gene Kelly fan. The tattoo guy says this to you. You think, there is nothing cooler than a guy with tattoos who loves Gene Kelly. You tell him that you were a Fred Astaire fan, that you took tap-dancing lessons when you were eleven. He tells you he was getting stoned and cutting school when he was eleven. At one point you notice that he's staring at the fish. He notices that you notice. He says, *I like to watch them sleep. See how they're all bunched up there together? Like it looks like they're watching us? That's them sleeping.* You love that he loves watching his fish sleep, even the one with the big brain-head. You imagine him watching you sleep, wondering if you catch a break from your own big brain-head when you sleep. (Your imaginary answer: Not usually.) You think, I want to be with someone who stops to watch the fish. Now is the time when you will have sex with him. You watch the whole movie.

After the movie you talk about god. He believes very strongly in a loving god. You believe very strongly that he should be making out with you right now. You want very badly to believe in god. Previously, in his presence, you have openly discussed your confusion about the god issue. What is it, is it here at all times, does it have facial hair, does it have a personality, why do bad things happen, if there is a god, why haven't I had sex in such a long time, and so on. He calls you *one of the complicated people.* He points out that you wear a small cross around your neck. You say you like religious imagery. He says, *So you think that's coincidental?* You say, *I do not know.* You ask how he knows for sure there's a god. He tells you he just does. He says, *I try to ask myself all those questions and it just doesn't go anywhere. I ask, Why do bad things happen, and there's no answer and I go about my day. I don't have to know. I'm being taken care of. I should be dead. I give props to the G-O-D, you know what I'm saying? I'm a simple guy. It's cool.* You like his simplicity. You are delighted for the refreshing change from months and years spent with guys who complicate things, who think complicated thoughts, who provide further complications for your preexisting complicated thoughts. You want to believe he's right. You want to believe that something so simple could be so right, could need no further examination from you. You wish you were a simple girl. You will take a simple guy.

You stay up late talking. He is not trying to have sex with you. You wonder if he is being gentlemanly. If he is waiting for later, *taking things slow.* You wonder if he understands that he could be having sex with you right now. You wonder why any guy in his right mind would not want to have sex with you right now. You decide it's time to go. He walks you to your car. He gives you a hug and a kiss on the cheek and a refrigerator magnet and a Charms Blow Pop.

You think, That was one of the top five best dates ever. You try to think of four others that even come close. You narrow it down to three, and that includes your first date ever, senior year, which makes the cut simply because you waited so long, and the date who played the piano and made you margaritas and read you Shakespeare assuming you'd understand (which was, at the time, a breakthrough). You call to say that you had a good time. You get voice mail. His message says something like, *Yo, keep shining.* He does not call back. When you finally run into him he seems neither interested nor uninterested. You call up some guy friends. You describe the date. The music, the candles, the flowers, the dinner, the Blow Pop. You say, *Was that a date? Maybe it wasn't a date.* All agree that it was a date. One laughs and says, *The only time I ever did that for a girl I asked her to marry me.* Another one says, *Maybe he's gay.* You enjoy the idea that the only reason someone would not try to have sex with you is because they're gay. You say, *He's not gay.* He asks if there was any physical contact. You tell him about the afghan. He says, *Shoes on or off?* You say, *Off.* He says, *Make no mistake. That was a date.* Another says, *Maybe he's intimidated by you.* People have said things like this before. You do not see yourself as intimidating in any way. You see yourself as pretty enough, smart enough, funny enough, neurotic enough, not overly anything. And he seems fairly confident, a not-easily-intimidated guy. You cannot figure out what went wrong or even if anything went wrong. There may be many reasons or there may be no reason. The reason may be that he is

Italian. That he *just likes candles.* That in his mind, romance doesn't have to mean romance. You're down with that except for the part about wanting the sex.

So you stop trying to figure it out. You let it go. You decide you will *Let go and let god.* You say to yourself, Maybe this is the only way god knows how to reach me. Maybe I am being taken care of. Maybe god knows I will not pick up his messages if the messenger isn't hot. Or maybe this is just god's way of showing me what a date should be like. Maybe god is talking to me now, saying, *It is my decree that you should expect love songs and flowers and candles and lollipops.* Maybe god is just trying to show me a model for all future dates. There is no other explanation.

Good for You!

SOMEONE FINALLY TOOK A PICTURE OF ME I don't hate and since I was wearing a red shirt I thought it would be the perfect holiday card. I made fifty copies and put a special nondenominational greeting on there (*Hey, Happy Holidays!* I thought the *Hey* gave it a personal touch) and sent them out. Then I started to get some cards back with some peculiar responses like, *Good for you!*, even though I hadn't written any news worth praising on that particular card and then I finally got an e-mail from someone who said she hoped she'd caught me before I sent too many out because she didn't want me to embarrass myself and I looked at the card again to see if I was exposed in some way or if the printers said, *Hey,*

Merry Christmas!, by accident. But the card was just right, and so I e-mailed her back and said I didn't understand what she meant and she e-mailed back that most people who send photos like that also have husbands or babies in the photo. I e-mailed her back again and said that I am not most people.

Acknowledgments

For their hard work and overwhelming enthusiasm, I am indebted to Alice Tasman and Reagan Arthur. A thousand thank-yous and blessings on both your heads.

For more of the same I'm grateful to Michael Mezzo and Geoff Shandler.

For early encouragement I thank Adam Langer.

For very early encouragement I thank Dick and Lois, Mark, Reed, Rob, and Susan.

Profound gratitude to Nina Solomon and Bob Leonard, who read all of these stories in their early stages, and whose friendship is, well, without them I would be in some trouble.

Adam Levin has also been an invaluable reader. He never lies, which is better than it sounds.

Sincere thanks to Rebecca Rauve from the *Sycamore Review* for making all the postage worth it. Thanks also to the Chicago Writers Group.

And to a few more friends/hipsterati whose contributions have been crucial (in the way of cakes, counsel, dinners, housing, photos, reading skills, and misc. trudging), I thank: Paige Barnes, Shauna Angel Blue, Michael Blum, David Boatman, Liz Cochran, Chris Geddes, Lisa Gerstein, Sue Haas, John Hannon, Alex Kemp, Peter Lear, Emily Mann, Mary Reagan, Jesse Ritter, Anne Roche, Eric Rosenblum, Karin Uz, Jackie Wolk.

When the Messenger Is Hot

STORIES BY

Elizabeth Crane

A Reading Group Guide

A Conversation with the Author of *When the Messenger Is Hot*

Elizabeth Crane talks with Adam Langer
for the *Chicago Tribune Magazine*'s
"On the Verge" column

When Elizabeth Crane turned forty in the spring of 2001, her best friend of nearly thirty years, Nina Solomon, flew in from New York and presented her with a gift: a blue long-sleeved, rhinestone-studded T-shirt with the word "FAMOUS" printed on it. The shirt proved to be prophetic. Six months later, Crane, who had spent the previous six years in Chicago piecing together a living as a preschool teacher and short story writer, signed a contract for her first collection of short stories, *When the Messenger Is Hot*, with Little, Brown and Co.

This month [January 2003], the newly published book began appearing in stores and Crane's life seems poised to undergo a sea change.

"I always knew she'd become famous doing something," says Solomon, a Manhattan schoolteacher who not long ago scored a book contract of her own for her first novel, *Single Wife*, with Algonquin

Books. "I figured she'd be a singer or an actress, but she's always been a hilarious writer too."

"I used to think that success was for other people," Crane, now forty-one, said recently, sipping a cappuccino in the Caffe De Luca near the intersection of Damen and North Avenues. Her getup was funky in a Wicker Park boutique sort of way — a white cardigan festooned with a floral pattern, a lime-green scarf also with flowers on it, blue jeans, boots. Her new shearling coat, the one extravagance she has allowed herself from her book contract, was heaped next to her in the booth; her movie-star sunglasses were tucked away in her bag. "I didn't think success was possible for me," she said. "I thought you had to have connections. I felt sort of persecuted or something."

Throughout her life, the Ukrainian Village resident has had near-brushes with fame. She was born in Johnson City, N.Y., the same city that produced author David Sedaris. After her parents separated when she was six, she lived in New York with her mother, who sang with the New York City Opera and performed opposite Luciano Pavarotti in *Rigoletto*. She went to high school at Columbia Prep with such future luminaries as actress Ally Sheedy, CNN legal analyst Jeffrey Toobin, and movie directors Eric Schaeffer (*My Life's in Turnaround*) and Gary Winick (*Tadpole*).

"A lot of people were making it early," Crane said wryly. "One of my greatest dreams has always been to have something worth putting in my high school newsletter."

After graduating in 1984 from the George Washington University with a degree in communications, she worked odd jobs in New York, waitressing, temping, teaching grade school as a substitute. At one of her lowest ebbs, she was working at a video store when a high school classmate, not knowing she was employed there, walked in, did a double-take, and asked her if she was going to their reunion. "Not now, I'm not," she told him.

Crane also worked as a talent booker, lining up child models for Sears and JC Penney — helping to launch the careers of tots twenty years younger than she. Her first decently paying job was as tutor to Macaulay Culkin's siblings in 1994 when Culkin starred in the John Hughes film *Richie Rich*, which was shot, in part, in Chicago. She worked here with the Culkins for six months while living at the Residence Inn by Marriott on Walton Street.

"They were fun, nice kids, and they had a tough family life," she recalls. She tutored the Culkins on and off in New York for about three years, then in July 1996 decided to move back to Chicago.

"I feel connected to this place," Crane says. "It was funny. After *Richie Rich*, I went back to New York and didn't work for a while and ran out of money and I got depressed. I'd see these movies and shows that were shot in Chicago and say, 'Ohhhhh, look, it's an el stop.' I thought about going back, but I thought, 'What am I going to do in Chicago?'"

Crane moved here anyway, and got a job as a nursery school teacher near the Cabrini-Green housing project. And for the first time, she began to write seriously. She had dabbled in screenplays, stories, and poems (growing up in a Manhattan apartment, one of her earliest efforts was a poem entitled "My Doorman Who Watches TV"), but only when she got to Chicago did she start submitting stories to magazines and working on a novel. "I really started coming into my own when I came here," she says.

The stories — quirky, smart, sometimes fantastical tales of women seeking to find successful relationships or escape bad ones — caught the attention of some literary editors. Like Crane, the stories were self-effacing, refreshingly unpretentious, and, even when dealing with topics such as losing a loved one to cancer (Crane's mother died of the disease in 1998), funny and true.

"Her writing has some heart. It's not all tricks and 24-carat words," says fellow Chicago writer Joe Meno, author of *How the Hula Girl Sings* and *Tender as Hellfire*.

While dating a number of men who all happened to have the same name, Crane penned a story, "The Daves," about a woman with just that experience. Another piece was written in the form of a personal ad placed by a woman to catch the eye of heartthrob actor Benicio Del Toro.

"I'm sort of tired of writing disastrous relationship stories," says Crane, who is single and sometimes, as she did in "The Daves," uses her dating misadventures as fodder for her fiction. "They're funny, but I would like to actually write about something that works out. And I would also like some experience to bring to that table. I find it really hard to write [a] relationship story that works out because it's impossible for me to imagine."

One of the first stories Crane wrote in Chicago, "The Archetype's Girlfriend" — a breathless, harried litany of bad girlfriend types that reads like a stand-up comedy monologue — wound up in the literary magazine *Washington Square*. Other tales were published in the *Florida Review* and *New York Stories*.

"Her voice completely knocked me out," says literary agent Alice Tasman, of the Jean Naggar Agency, which represents such bestselling novelists as Jean Auel and Tony Hillerman. Tasman signed Crane on the basis of just a few stories and the manuscript for an unfinished novel, something she says she rarely does. "Her writing was a blast of energy that I hadn't seen in so long. . . . I think she could be huge."

When Crane finally got her book deal in November of 2001, she celebrated modestly. She had dinner with a few friends, sent out a slew of enthusiastic e-mails, and that was that. "It was very low-key," she says. "My life was not changed in any dramatic way. I was still eating macaroni and cheese."

But if things go the way Crane's agent and publisher plan, she could wind up being the next big artist to emerge from Chicago. Little, Brown has printed 25,000 copies of *When the Messenger Is Hot*, a significant number for a first-time short story writer. Tasman compares Crane to the writers Pam Houston (*Cowboys Are My Weakness*) and Aimee Bender (*The Girl in the Flammable Skirt*). Her editor, Reagan Arthur, who outbid another major publishing house to sign Crane, invokes the names of David Foster Wallace (*Brief Interviews with Hideous Men*) and edgy, iconoclastic singer-songwriter Syd Straw.

But if there's one person whose Crane's stories most recall, it may be another female Chicago artist who has written cleverly, knowingly, and introspectively about bad relationships and loneliness, an artist who can blend tragedy, comedy, and irony in one sentence, who also is given to wearing funky duds and hanging out in bars and cafes in Bucktown and Wicker Park: Liz Phair.

"Wow," Crane says when the comparison is made. She laughs, tosses her hair, and beams. "Wow," she says again. "Listen, you can compare me to a rock star anytime."

Adam Langer is a playwright and former writer and critic for the Chicago Reader. *He is the senior editor of* Book *magazine, which published Elizabeth Crane's story "The Daves." His article on Elizabeth Crane, entitled "When the Writer Is Hot," appeared in the* Chicago Tribune Magazine *on January 26, 2003. Reprinted with permission.*

Reading Group Questions and Topics for Discussion

1. Why do you think the author chose to open the collection with "The Archetype's Girlfriend"? Which of the character traits described in the story apply to you? Your friends?

2. What does "Something Shiny" say about identity? How easily can others "figure us out"? Do you think, like Apple Fowler, there is someone who might be able to live your life better than you?

3. How do the fantastical elements in "Privacy and Coffee," "Something Shiny," "Return from the Depot!" and "The Daves" help illustrate the characters' emotional lives? How do you think the stories might have played out in reality?

4. Why does the narrator in "Privacy and Coffee" become a recluse? Is it possible to completely cut one-

self off from the world? Where would you set up camp if you could pick any place in the world? How long do you think you'd be happy there?

5. Why do you think the author chose to write "You Take Naps" and "When the Messenger Is Hot" in the second person? How does this approach affect your understanding of the stories?

6. What do you think Alice is trying to express through her poem at the end of "An Intervention"? Is her poem good or bad? Does it make a difference either way? How might the story be different without it?

7. Which character in the collection changes the most by the end of her story? Which character changes the least? Which character's decisions do you most agree with? Disagree with?

8. The concept of "denial" has left the therapist's office and entered mainstream conversation. Which stories in this collection deal with denial? Does the author seem wholeheartedly to condemn or endorse it?

9. Why do you think the author included so many footnotes in "The Super Fantastic New Zealand Triangle"? If you could footnote your life, what would need the most explaining?

10. In "Christina," is the ghost baby real or just a figment of the narrator's imagination? What does Christina represent?

On the Subject of Influences Blatant, Less Blatant, Random, or Otherwise

AN ESSAY BY

Elizabeth Crane

Here's my whole thing about influences by way of a disclaimer: I wouldn't dare compare myself to any of the following people (nor do I imagine anyone else would), whose books I bow before nightly in solemn prayer. As a writer, whatever ends up inspiring you, you hope that your writing is its own thing, heretofore unprecedented in its uniqueness. That said, do I occasionally shamelessly rip people off? Er, yeah. Am I thoroughly inspired to write by books I love? Of course. Am I inspired by things that have nothing to do with books at all, like babies who seem to be speaking to me telepathically or songs by Pete Yorn or movies that could have been better? Often. Whether or not any of these things are necessarily reflected in my work probably isn't for me to decide.

So but okay, I should start by saying, by confessing, that for years, I read a lot of — how to be kind —

trashy novels, and I watched soap operas, and went to see movies like *Roller Boogie.* It's true. I had always loved reading and went to a pretty nice prep school in Manhattan, where we were assigned some really great books that were often way too advanced for our reading levels. (e.g., *Cat's Cradle* by Kurt Vonnegut in sixth grade, which I loved, in spite of having no comprehension of what it was about, for the language and the character names and lists. My friends and I briefly formed a religion, with text, inspired by the book, centered on the wearing of a particular style of buckled loafer.) We read *The Catcher in the Rye* the following year too, which I'm sure I didn't fully understand either, but loved just the same. (Later on, in spite of the excellence of the reading lists, I'd be skipping a lot of the reading assignments. I had a big thing then, and still do, about reading something I have to read. So if I ever read, say, *Ulysses*, it will likely be because it randomly got into my head that I wanted to. But don't count on a book report on that anytime soon.) In any case, somewhere along the line, I started reading these trashy epics, and as I tend to be a little slow on the mark in nearly every aspect of my life, it took me a number of years to get bored (with those and the soaps, too) and realize I was essentially reading the same book over and over with different names and locations. Sometimes I even knew what the next line would be. The unfortunate thing was that I hadn't found anything to replace it with that really floated my boat. Until. Almost thirteen years ago I found myself temping in the literary department of a talent agency in New York and someone handed me a copy of *The Broom of the System*. Boat in float. Boat up and out of the water and circling overhead. So.

Re: shameless off-ripping. For years I've been blathering about my love for all things David Foster Wallace to anyone who would listen. Now I get to carry my message of hope nationwide. There's a ten-page story in my collection with nineteen footnotes — or maybe I should call it nineteen footnotes with a ten-page story — and I'd be flat-out lying if I said I woke up one morning and came up with this genius idea of where to put all my tangential thoughts. (I had always been fond of parentheses [and brackets!], but to me this use of footnotes was revolutionary.) Yet in spite of the footnotes, and the long sentences, and the parens., and sentences that begin with *But* or *So* or *Anyway* or *And* or any and all of the above, I don't anticipate a comparison anytime soon. For me, pinpointing influences is a more nebulous exercise. From the time *TBOTS* fell into my hands, and *Infinite Jest* and numerous books by other authors, I began to see that it was okay, possibly even a good thing, to break rules (which had been tripping me up in a major way; for one thing, I felt compelled to try to describe things specifically in a physical way, settings in particular, but sometimes people too, and honestly, I suck at straightforward descriptions of trees and such, not to mention that things like that didn't seem relevant enough to my universe, trees, having grown up in NY — not that I couldn't just as well describe buildings, except for that I couldn't, and I've always been much more interested in getting right to the characters anyway, and so with regard to any kind of description, I think I'm more interested than anything in some little detail about a person that seems to say a million things: for example, I don't think my agent will mind too much if I tell you that she doesn't carry a purse — I haven't ever written anything about her, but the point is, it's of endless fascination to me, several years later, that a high-powered New York agent wouldn't need some kind of a bag to carry around all her agency things — note use of "agency" as adjective, as evidence of my describing problem — that anyone, agents aside, could be so carefree that they don't carry around a bag full of stuff just in case, like me, and so it of course follows that she doesn't wear makeup [and doesn't need to, and therefore does not also need, in the bag she doesn't carry, a bag inside the bag, full of makeup] and so you see, given those two little bits of information, you can elicit that Alice is a naturally pretty, low-maintenance-type person), that there was room for me to write the way I thought people sounded (or thought) in real life, often rambling and sometimes with a dearth of periods but hopefully always coming back around and making sense as a whole, in the end. (But you know, draw your own conclusions about that when you're finished with this essay.) This would later be confirmed for me reading anything and everything by (to name only a few) Lydia Davis, Rick Moody, Lorrie Moore, George Saunders (whose work I'm so madly in love with it pains me) and continues with the blessed likes of Aimee Bender, Arthur Bradford, and Gabe Hudson (even though his book, *Dear Mr. President,* came out after mine was completed — but in the unlikely event that I write anything vaguely war-related in the future, you'll know how the inspiration struck). With regard to Saunders, Bradford, and Bender, I was reminded that when I was quite a bit younger, many of my stories had fantastical elements: in junior high I'd written a novella about a fictional creature called a Gerfl that lived under the dining room table (props to my sister Susan, who was about four at the time and originated the Gerfl as part of a game), and in college I wrote what might be called a young adult novel about a baby born in an empty room whose goal is (ostensibly) to get onto the Johnny Carson show (in fact she's really looking for her parents). And so after reading stories like Bradford's "Dogs," in which a man has an, um, improper relationship with his girlfriend's dog (resulting in the birth of a litter of puppies and one small dogchild), I was moved to bring elements of fantasy into my own work again, as in "Christina," a story about a woman whose roommate is a ghost baby, or "Return from the Depot!," in which the narrator's mother comes back from the dead and becomes a sitcom star. (Sidebar: a nice bonus of writing is that you can bring people you love back from the dead, at least on the page. To the best of my knowledge, however, my mom is not in fact living in L.A. with her new husband Alan Thicke.) Regardless of whether any of these influences come through in my writing, at the very least, it's safe to say that my reading habits have changed dramatically for the better.

But I still like a good B movie every now and again.

This essay first appeared at Powells.com. Reprinted with permission.

About the Author

Elizabeth Crane's work has appeared in the *Sycamore Review, Washington Square, New York Stories, Book,* the *Florida Review, Eclipse, Chicago Reader, Sonora Review, Wisconsin Review,* and *Bridge Magazine.* She lives in Chicago and teaches writing at Northwestern University.